MW00888014

Praise for Stephen Russell Payne's **Ties That** ~~Bind Us~~

"Peopled with characters that openly disdain the postcard Vermont, the stories of Stephen Russell Payne plumb the depths of rural hardship, farm life and small dreams. Thanks to Payne's unerring eye for detail and ear for voice, these stories turn modest lives into treasure, by revealing the tenderness that makes them possible."
  —Stephen Kiernan, author of *The Curiosity and The Hummingbird*

"Stephen Russell Payne's short story collection is a spectacular debut by a writer who knows his characters, the state of Vermont, and the frailties of human beings caught up in the mortal coil; he does it all with grace, depth, intimacy, and at times a sly sense of humor. I loved these stories."
  —Ernest Hebert, author of *The Dogs of March* from the *Darby Series*

Stephen Russell Payne's new short story collection is a terrific piece of work. Payne is a fourth generation Vermonter and knows his kinsmen well. His stories bring to life – not in the voice of an omniscient narrator – but in the voices of those living them, Vermont's hardscrabble past. Payne leads us into an earlier Vermont, replete with durable characters – both in their own lives and in our memory.
  —Bill Schubart, author of *Panhead* and many short story collections

Stephen Russell Payne's new collection of stories, *Ties That Bind Us,* takes us far off the interstates, ski slopes, and upscale bed-and-breakfasts and microbreweries to the backroads, backwoods, and half-abandoned former mill towns of a Vermont most visitors to the Green Mountain State don't know exists. His wonderfully independent-minded characters are the very last of a breed, whose like will not be seen again. These stories, written with clear-eyed affection, gentle humor, and great expertise, remind me of *Country of the Pointed Firs*. They are a loving exploration of a unique but vanishing place and its noble people, who know better than anyone that their way of life is fading fast.

—Howard Frank Mosher, award winning author of *God's Kingdom*

No one writes with as much passion and insight about northern Vermont as Stephen Russell Payne. With the meticulousness of a surgeon, and the lyricism of a poet, Payne captures the tenacity and honesty of the denizens of the Green Mountain State's small towns and villages. Reading Payne is like a visit from a good old friend. His tales are always infused with equal measures of humor, wisdom, and love.

—Jennifer Finny Boylan, best-selling author of *She's Not There*

Stephen Russell Payne's short stories have shown him to be among New England's finest writers of regional fiction. We believe in these characters and care about them. Payne is in top form.

—X. J. Kennedy, Winner of the *Robert Frost Medal for Poetry*

Ties That
Bind Us

Ties That Bind Us

A Collection of Vermont Short Stories

STEPHEN RUSSELL PAYNE

Cedar Ledge Publishing

ISBN: 1534792163
ISBN 13: 9781534792166
Library of Congress Control Number: 2016914420
CreateSpace Independent Publishing Platform
North Charleston, South Carolina
Publisher's Cataloging-in-Publication Data
Payne, Stephen
Ties That Bind Us, A Collection of Vermont Short Stories / Stephen Payne
1. Vermont – Fiction 2. New England - Fiction

Manufactured in the United States of America

For information, permissions and appearances, please visit our website, www.StephenRussellPayne.com, or Facebook at Stephen Russell Payne.

Cedar Ledge Publishing

Also by
STEPHEN RUSSELL PAYNE

Cliff Walking — A Novel
Riding My Guitar-The Rick Norcross Story

To
My Friend and Mentor

Howard Frank Mosher

A great American writer
Whose generosity knows no bounds

Acknowledgements

Growing up in Vermont's Northeast Kingdom, the people I was most attracted to were storytellers of one sort or another. I'm grateful for the way they colored the 'real' world, making it more understandable, entertaining, and often more meaningful. By their fictional nature, short stories allow us 'psychic distance' through which we can experience a more honest look at ourselves and where we come from; a more critical view of our social history and traditions. Living in the Kingdom gave me a lifetime of fascinating people and places from which to draw complex, engaging characters.

I fondly remember one fellow in particular, a local Grange member and junk dealer named, Howard McKinstry. Back in the 1960's he'd arrive in his old pickup just about the time my mother would be serving lunch. His rusty Ford overflowing with treasures, Howard would emerge from behind the wheel, as spent oil cans, and pieces of salvaged brass and copper invariably rolled out of the cab with him. He would stand at our front porch and bellow through the screen door: "Louise, come out of there; I got a great bargain for you today!" Truth was, we procured many a fine antique from Howard, but more importantly, we delighted in his visits, as he entertained us around our kitchen table with often-hysterical renditions of his rural exploits. A thoroughbred Vermonter, Howard was one of the first people who got me interested in telling stories, and I've been doing it ever since.

I want to express appreciation to Tom Slayton, Editor Emeritus of *Vermont Life Magazine*, who published my first story about my Dad's deer camp in Irasburg, Vermont, up near the Canadian Border. Tom's journalistic tutelage over many years taught me a great deal about how to write good stories.

To the many thoughtful readers who have critiqued these and other stories, sincere thanks. To Marietta, my wife, and ever-patient *First Reader,* you have taught me so much in so many ways. I thank you and I love you. And finally, sincere appreciation to my longtime editor, Lesley Kellas Payne of Fresno, California. I simply would not be on this wonderful literary journey without your twenty years of caring, insightful guidance.

Several of these stories have been previously published. "The Dixon Brothers," "Sunday at the Dump," and "Trips to the Woodshed," have appeared in the *Vermont Literary Review.* "End of the Season," and "Executive Session" appeared in *Route 7 - A Vermont Literary Journal.*

Contents

Chapter 1

The Dixon Brothers

"Willie, put your teeth in. We got to go."

Willie rubbed his ear into his hunched-up shoulder then looked at his brother, Wendell. "I ain't goin'."

"What do you mean, you ain't going?"

Willie frowned as he pushed himself out of his chair, stained gauze pads scattering to the floor. He steadied himself with his cane then limped out of the parlor into the kitchen, favoring his left leg, the one with the chronic ulcers.

Wendell stepped into the doorway. "Now don't be getting that way. We're just doing what I promised."

"*I* never promised," Willie said, tapping the metal ash pan beneath the wood stove with his cane.

"Willie, we been over it a hundred times. You was too young. I promised for you."

"Ma shoulda' talked to me."

"You was only eight when Ma died. And a little hellion. There wan't no talking to you."

"Was that after I got hurt?"

"Yes, you fell outta' the barn on your head the year before, when you were seven." Wendell shook his head. "Should of taken care of this years ago. We're too old now; minds aren't sharp. This is just what Ma worried about."

"I don't like it, Wendell. This thing scares me."

Wendell stepped over to his little brother. "Mr. Martin's a nice man. He'll make it easy for us."

Willie's face tightened with concern.

"What is it?" Wendell asked.

"I ain't scared of going to see Mr. Martin." He stared at the deeply worn, wide pine floor boards. "I just don't want to be left alone."

Wendell put his arm around Willie's shoulders. "Don't worry, one way or the other we'll always be together."

"How do you know?"

"Well, Ma told me. And Reverend Cummings said so, too, right from his Sunday pulpit." He looked into Willie's droopy eyes. "Ma's still here, sort of. You know. Some nights we talk to her at the supper table, just like she was eating with us. It'll be the same for you and me. Don't matter who goes first."

"I guess. But it's different with you. You're my brother."

"I know." Wendell motioned toward the sink. "Now let's get your teeth in. We don't want Mr. Martin waiting on us."

Willie pulled away. "I'll go on one account."

"What's that?"

"You read me Huck Finn tonight."

Wendell nodded. "'Course I will, like always."

Willie hobbled over, took hold of the linoleum counter and leaned against the scratched porcelain sink. A single red geranium stood in a clay pot on the chipped white paint of the windowsill. Afternoon sunlight lit the patchy stubble of Willie's face as his crooked fingers wedged yellowed dentures into his mouth. He chomped down a couple times, wiping a gob of adhesive on his pants. Then he leaned on his cane and headed for the front door. Wendell followed him outside to their rusted Dodge Power Wagon as several chickens scattered across the otherwise abandoned farmyard.

Standing by the truck, Willie raised his cane toward the tractor shed, its roof split in two from decades of heavy winter snows. "If we don't get after that it's goinna' crush the hood of the Deere." For a few moments they stared at the faded green tractor they'd driven over their farm's rocky fields for better than half a century.

"Yup," Wendell said, opening Willie's door. "We'll get after that." He boosted Willie up onto his seat then forced the door shut with his shoulder. He walked around to the driver's side, slid an old boat cushion over a protruding spring, and climbed in. He pulled out the choke, pumped the gas pedal, and fired it up. The sweet smell of exhaust soon filled the cab. When the engine settled, Wendell took hold of the stick shift with both hands. Having been frozen in four-wheel-drive for years, the transmission moaned like a downed cow as he ground it into first gear. He gave it some gas and they lurched forward out of the yard onto the road.

Given its questionable brakes, Wendell kept the Dodge in second gear as they descended the winding dirt road lined with grand old maples and broken runs of barbed wire. Halfway down the hill, they passed Ray Nelson's sugar woods.

Willie sat up straighter. "Just look at them blue lines running through the woods." He shook his head. "Lazy is all. Buckets the only way to catch sap. Plastic pipe ruins the flavor, ties the trees all up in knots. They's supposed to be free, ain't they, Wendell?"

Wendell nodded. "Yes, but hardly anyone gathers by hand anymore."

Below Nelson's, Willie pointed to a collection of tin sap buckets hanging at odd angles on a stand of large maples. "Ivan's still got buckets up," he said. "Snow's gone, trees all budded out. He ought to have them down and washed by now."

"I guess I forgot to tell you that one night a few weeks back, Ivan's old lady brought a baked bean supper up to the sugar house and found him slumped dead against the woodpile, syrup all burned to hell. Too bad, that was a sweet run of sap."

"Well, his buckets ought to be down anyway."

"Willie—the poor guy's dead."

"No excuse."

Wendell shook his head, forced the truck into third gear and headed into town.

"Wendell," Willie said, as they passed Lester's Texaco.

"What is it?"

"Can I ask you a question—I mean later?"

"'Course. Ask it now if you want."

"C'ain't."

"Why not?"

"It's private."

Wendell looked around the cab. "This isn't private enough?"

"Nope. We's in town."

"Suit yourself."

Willie stared out the window as they drove down Main Street, visibly tensing as Wendell steered into the parking lot of Martin's Funeral Home.

"Ready?"

Willie crossed his arms. "I ain't goin' in."

"Yes you are."

Willie reached down, pulled his pant leg up over his knee and scratched around the blistered edges of his ulcers. "What if they's, you know, a dead one in there?"

"We're not here to see no dead people. Besides, we'll just be in the show-room, or whatever they call it."

Wendell got out and opened Willie's door. He pulled Willie's pant leg back down then helped him out of the truck and over to the front entrance. Wendell held the heavy door as Willie hobbled over the threshold into a foyer paneled with dark wood. Navy blue carpet covered the floor. The door closed behind them, shutting out all sounds from the street.

Willie sniffed the air. "Smells strange in here."

"Kind of musty," Wendell said, looking around. "Wonder where Mr. Martin is."

"They's a light on down there," Willie said, pointing to the end of the foyer.

They walked past a tall brass vase full of purple gladiolas to a doorway framed with heavy maroon drapes.

"This place is creepy," Willie said. "I'm gettin' outta' here."

"Not till we're done our business, you aren't. Now come on." Wendell took Willie's sleeve and led him through the doorway into a room filled with rows of chairs, in front of which sat an open casket.

"Shit worth a damn!" Willie exclaimed, grabbing hold of Wendell's arm. "You said we wouldn't see no dead people."

"We aren't in the right place." Wendell turned away. "Let's go back outside. Must be another door where the live customers come in."

Willie didn't budge. He just stared at the corpse.

"Come on, now."

"Ain't that Horace?" Willie said, limping down the aisle toward the casket.

"You get away from there."

Willie peered over the side of the casket at the head of the corpse. "Yes sir, Horace Bagley in the flesh. What's he doing here?"

Wendell walked down the aisle and peered over Willie's shoulder. "For cryin' out loud, Willie, he's dead."

"Looks kinda' peaceful, don't he?"

Wendell looked at Horace's face. "They musta' done something to him. He's clean shaven for God's sake."

"Mr. Dixon?"

Wendell looked back, recognized the elderly man in a black suit walking down the aisle. "Mr. Martin—"

"Nice to see you again," Mr. Martin said, shaking Wendell's hand. He turned. "And you must be Willie."

Willie shook hands without looking at him.

"Did you folks know Horace? He was a fine horseshoe player."

Wendell nodded. "We used to play Saturdays behind the Grange Hall. He had a good arm."

Mr. Martin smiled. "Now, if you gentlemen will follow me, I'll take you downstairs to go over things."

Willie turned back to Horace. "Can you make *anyone* look this good?"

"Usually," Mr. Martin said. "My granddaughter does an excellent job with the cosmetic work."

Willie pointed at Horace's face. "What's that red stuff? Don't look like a man ought to."

"Rouge. Puts a little color in their cheeks."

"His cheeks were never that color."

"Well they are now," Wendell said. "Now come on, follow Mr. Martin."

Willie frowned at Wendell then followed them down a narrow staircase into a showroom displaying several different styles of coffins. A heavy oak desk stood on one side of the room, over which hung a large black and white photograph of a crowd of people at a railroad station. A banner laid out on the lawn in front of them read: "The People of St. Johnsbury – 1928."

Mr. Martin led them over to the desk. He motioned to a pair of captain's chairs. "Please sit down."

Wendell looked up at the photograph. "Will you look at that," he said. "Mr. Jenks took that when we was kids."

"Do you remember that day?" Mr. Martin asked.

Wendell raised his wire-rimmed glasses up onto his forehead. "Yes, sir. We was there with Ma and Grandpa Amos. Watched the Calvin Coolidge steam in from Morrisville on the St. J. & LC, newest locomotive in Vermont." He pointed. "Right there, with two American flags flying off the boiler."

Willie straightened as much as his arthritis would allow.

"Can you see?" Wendell asked.

"Not really."

"Here," Mr. Martin said. "Let's we take it down for you."

He lifted the photograph off its hook and laid it on the desk. Willie leaned over the dusty glass.

"Do you remember being in this picture?" Mr. Martin asked.

"Nope."

"They took a lot of pictures that day," Wendell said, as he looked over the somewhat faded photograph. "I remember them telling us to stand still, hold our breath as long as we could so as not to blur the negative. It was hard for Ma and Grandpa 'cause they were so sick, just kept coughing." Wendell pointed to a woman holding a young boy. Another, older boy stood at her side. Behind her was an elderly man with a long white beard whose hand rested on her shoulder.

Wendell pointed. "See that blurry kid? That's you, right there in Ma's arms. You never stayed still for a second."

Willie slid his crooked fingertips across the glass. "That's Ma and me?" he asked, a deep reverence in his voice.

"Sure is. I'm beside her and Grandpa Amos behind. Ma took him out of the home to go down for the town picture."

"Outta' what home?"

"The County Home for the sick. Grampa had consumption. You know that."

"They take this picture before I fell outta' the barn?"

Wendell glanced uncomfortably at Mr. Martin. "You're about three in this picture. You was seven when you had the accident."

Willie squinted at his image under the glass. "So I was normal then?"

"Yes. You was a rascal, but normal."

"I'll be darned," Willie said, raising his hand to his chin.

Mr. Martin slid the picture to the side of the desk. "Well, we'd better get started." He opened a file then looked over his bifocals at Wendell. "Before your mother died she set aside enough money so that you and Willie wouldn't have to worry about your final arrangements. She talked to me about—"

"You talked to Ma?" Willie interjected.

"Yes, several times. She told me what she wanted for you boys." Mr. Martin shook his head. "Terrible to die so young, but back in those days they didn't have good treatments for sugar diabetes. Poor thing was almost blind when her kidneys finally failed."

"Was she pretty?" Willie asked.

"Your mother was very pretty, and kind. She didn't want the same thing to happen to you and Wendell that happened to your grandfather Amos."

"What happened to him?"

Wendell slid forward on his chair. "I'm sorry, Mr. Martin, Willie's memory's bad. I've told him a hundred times."

"It's all right." Mr. Martin folded his hands on the desk. "Willie, your grandfather was a hard-working farmer. He put enough food on the table but wasn't able to save any money. When he took sick your mother was left alone working the farm, raising you boys. Not well herself, the best she could do was put Amos in the County Home. When he died she couldn't afford a funeral so they buried him out back in a pauper's grave, no stone of his own. She wanted you boys to have better."

Mr. Martin paused for a few moments. "So what we need to do today is pick out a casket for each of you and a memorial you can share."

"Do we get a funeral?" Willie asked.

"You could have a small service if you wish."

"I'd like that," Wendell said.

"Do you belong to a church, have some friends or relatives still living?"

Wendell thought for a moment. "No church, but we've got a cousin up in East Burke, and a couple fellows from the grange might come."

"That would be fine. We could have a little service here." Mr. Martin pushed his chair back. "Now let's look at a casket."

They followed Mr. Martin toward the back of the room. Willie stopped beside a heavily-lacquered mahogany model. He slid his hand along its polished brass rail then peered inside, pushed on the thick cushioned silk with the hook of his cane. "Here's a dandy one."

Wendell stepped closer.

Willie rapped his knuckles on the curved top. "Solid." He looked up and down the length of it. "It's long enough. We'd fit."

Wendell reached in, felt the white silk ruffle then shook his head. "This isn't right for us." He looked over at Mr. Martin. "Got anything less fancy?"

"Certainly. Come this way." He motioned to a simple, square-topped casket sitting against the back wall.

Wendell and Willie walked over and ran their hands over the smooth wood planks forming the box. Wendell examined the corner of the lid. "Good tight tongue and groove."

"A lot of farmers choose this one," Mr. Martin said.

"Nice wide pine," Willie said. "And it don't have that frilly stuff." He stretched his arms out, hooking his fingers around the end of the box. "You don't suppose we'd both fit in one?"

"Kind of a two-fer," Wendell said.

"I don't think that would be possible." Mr. Martin placed his hand on top of the box. "So, you'd each like one of these?"

Wendell nodded.

Willie bent forward and rubbed his thigh. "I got to set down, Wendell. My leg's hurtin' awful."

Mr. Martin motioned back toward his desk. "Let's sit down. You can select a headstone and you'll be done."

Wendell helped Willie back to a chair. His ankle was swollen, and yellow fluid was streaking down his shin into his shoe.

Willie slumped into the chair. "I ain't got enough energy to pick me out a stone."

Mr. Martin opened a photo album. "Perhaps you could look through these sample pictures while you rest." He slid the photo album in front of them and turned through a few pages.

"Looky that one," Willie said, pointing to a shiny gray stone with a tractor engraved on it. "How'd they do that?"

"They've got a fancy laser at the monument company in Barre that can engrave most any design."

"That's it," Willie said, his eyes brightening. "We'll have the John Deere on ours."

Wendell smiled. "Good idea."

Mr. Martin didn't look so enthusiastic. "I'm sorry, but I don't think your Mother's account would cover that large a stone, or the engraving. Custom memorials are quite expensive."

Willie hung his head.

"Then any stone'll do," Wendell said.

"Well, let's say we get you boys a piece of Vermont granite and put both your names on it."

"I got to go home," Willie said, scratching at his leg.

Mr. Martin looked over the desk and frowned. "That looks terribly sore. Can I get you a bandage?"

"Nope. Needs air."

"We'll dress it when we get back to the farm," Wendell said.

"No more dressings." Willie suddenly stood. "Come on, Wendell. Goinna' get chilly tonight. We got to tend the stove."

Wendell stood.

Mr. Martin stepped around the side of his desk. "There is one other thing I should mention to you. There's always the option of cremation. Then you don't need to worry about a casket and all. People often have their ashes scattered over a special place."

Willie's eyes opened wide. "You mean burn us all to hell in one of them ovens? No goddamn way!" He got his cane under him and hurried toward an exit door.

"Mr. Dixon, that's not the way out."

Before Mr. Martin could stop him, Willie pushed the panic bar and fled. Wendell followed him outside into the back where old wooden shipping pallets and broken headstones protruded at odd angles from the grass. At the side of a dirt driveway, a black 1950s Cadillac hearse sat in a sea of overgrown raspberry bushes.

Wendell took after Willie, catching him at the end of the driveway.

"Willie!" Wendell took his arm. "Stop. We got to rest a minute."

"Truck's this way," Willie said. He leaned forward on his cane and shuffled up a slight incline to the parking lot, favoring his bad leg almost to the point of dragging it. When they reached the Dodge, they both leaned against the tailgate and caught their breath.

"Let's get out of here," Willie said, straightening up.

Wendell helped him into the truck then climbed in himself and they left.

As they drove out of town, dark storm clouds pushed into the Connecticut River valley from the north. Neither one spoke until they were safely back on their hill. As they climbed toward the turnoff to their farm, Willie turned to Wendell. "Can we keep going? Up to the old pasture."

Wendell tapped the fuel gauge causing the needle to bounce. "I 'spose we've got enough gas." He glanced at Willie. "But I'm worried about your leg. Besides, aren't you tired?"

"Yeah, but I like the view up there. It's peaceful."

"Okay."

They continued to the top of the hill where the road turned into nothing more than a set of old skidder ruts.

"Hang on." The transmission whined as Wendell downshifted into first.

Willie braced himself against the dash as they lurched forward, blackberry bushes scratching along the doors. After bouncing in the ruts for a few minutes, they broke out into a meadow of spring grass carpeted with brilliant yellow dandelions. They headed down across the meadow, driving past a line of retired apple trees to the far end of the field.

Wendell pulled to a stop at the edge of a steep drop off where a wide green valley opened below them like a great theater. In the distance, the snowcaps of the White Mountains of neighboring New Hampshire were illuminated with a warm yellow-purple glow from the setting sun.

Wendell rolled down his window, letting in cool Canadian air arriving ahead of the storm. "Just look at all them shades of green."

Willie nodded. "I want to be buried right here."

"Sounds good to me."

The sky darkened as clouds gathered against the mountains.

Wendell turned to his brother. "Back in town you wanted to ask me a question. This private enough?"

Willie stared out the windshield. "You ever had relations with a woman?"

Wendell adjusted his hands on the steering wheel. "Once."

"Who?"

"Rachael. Captain Smith's daughter."

"Why didn't you marry her?"

"Didn't want to."

"Why not?"

"I was busy keeping the farm."

Willie paused. "Did you love her?"

"I had a fancy for her."

Willie looked Wendell in the eye. "You let her go on account of me?"

Wendell paused, squinted. "Well, sort of, I guess."

The first raindrops splattered on the hood of the cab.

Willie looked down, scratched the edges of his sores. "I fear I've been a burden."

Wendell reached over, laid his hand on Willie's forearm. "Never."

Willie nodded without looking up. "Thank you, Wendell. Let's go home."

Wendell patted Willie's hand, turned the truck around and crossed back over the meadow. As they headed down the hill, rain fell harder on the roof of the Dodge.

Back at the farmhouse, a long black car pulled into the yard behind them. Wendell squinted at the approaching headlights. "Who could that be?"

Wearing a slicker, Mr. Martin got out of his Buick and walked over to Wendell. "I want you and your brother to have this," he said, handing Wendell a cardboard tube. "Good night, now." He touched the brim of his hat, walked back to his car and drove off.

With the tube under his arm, Wendell helped Willie out of the truck and into the kitchen where he collapsed in his chair. His breathing was labored, his forehead beaded with sweat.

"I'll make some hot tea," Wendell said, struggling to get Willie out of his damp coat.

"I'll tend the fire," Willie said in a whisper.

Wendell carefully tucked a gray army blanket around Willie's shoulders, and then turned to the woodstove. He shifted the damper then swung open the creaky front door, its glass heavily laden with black soot. He took a handful of wood shavings and a couple small pieces of birch, and set them on the few remaining hot embers. He leaned in and blew on the coals which glowed bright red. The shavings began to smoke then quickly caught fire. He left the firebox door open to warm the kitchen.

Wendell stepped to the sink and for a few moments enjoyed the familiar patter of rain on the kitchen windowpanes. He filled the kettle with water and set it on the stove. He stoked the fire again then sat at the table and opened the cardboard tube. He unrolled a large paper and held it at arm's length. Across the top of a sketch of a 1941 John Deere was a hand-written note which Wendell read out loud. "To Wendell and Willie. Hope this looks enough like yours. I've taken care of having it engraved for you. Sincerely, John Martin."

Wendell held up the sketch. "Look what Mr. Martin done for us. He's going to put the Deere on our stone."

Willie managed a weak smile.

Wendell set the sketch on the table, walked to the Hoosier and brought down a tackle box filled with Willie's dressings. He gently slid Willie's pant leg up over his knee and was alarmed at what he saw. Willie's lower leg had become a mottled purple color, with bright red streaks running up his thigh from the festered ulcers. There was an odor Wendell hadn't smelled before. "Dear God, we've got to get this cleaned up."

In his sleepiness, Willie tried to push him away. "Let it go," he mumbled, his dentures dislodging as he spoke.

"It's okay, little brother. Go back to sleep."

Wendell bent forward, pulled Willie's dentures from his mouth and set them in a saucer on the table. He tested the temperature of the water with his finger then poured it over a clean towel into a mixing bowl. He stirred in a tablespoon of Epsom salts and set it on the floor next to Willie's chair. Wendell knelt down, wrung out the towel and carefully washed around the edges of the ulcers.

When Wendell was finished, he wrapped Willie's leg with clean muslin then sat in his rocker, leaned back and rested. After a few minutes he picked up their mother's tattered copy of *Huckleberry Finn*, opened it to the strand of rawhide marking Willie's favorite passage, and began to read.

Chapter 2

Sunday at the Dump

Smoky Latrell opened the door of the *Cat House*, where he slept with Ellie, the 1960's Caterpillar bucket loader he used to crush and disperse piles of trash at the Clydesville town dump, a huge hollow dug out of the old Knapp farm a half century before. Every morning except Sunday, Smoky sorted through piles of junk thrown from the backs of pickups and station wagons. He'd pull out the treasures then bulldoze over the dump's rumpled surface, leaving behind a mosaic of his community's discarded lives. A square red kitchen clock from the forties, edges swiped with layers of old wall paint, its hands frozen when the new clock was hung. Superman comic books and newspapers, probably read only once, jammed with dented Campbell soup cans and empty ketchup and pickle bottles into a wooden produce box sporting a bright *California Navel Oranges* label.

Smoky stepped into the pink light of sunrise and surveyed the dump, a homemade toothpick protruding from a permanent indentation in his lower lip. He thought he'd heard something out there during the night. Not just the usual raccoons. Something bigger, an unusual rustling. Coydogs maybe. Once in a while they came in for dinner in the spring while waiting for mother rabbits to deliver their delicious young bunnies. Too quiet for a black bear. They grunted and sniffed, made a helluva mess clawing around, freeloading off bags of kitchen garbage hidden in the debris. Wasn't kids. When they came down on Saturday nights they'd stumble around, fart and belch beer, all the while laughing and shushing each other.

Last night's noise was different. It roused Smoky enough that he pushed himself up on his good elbow so he could peer out the window beside his army cot. But he was too foggy from drinking a mix of booze bottle remnants to get a clear bead on where the noise was coming from. Besides, he'd thought, thumping back down on his cot, he was too old to keep chasing varmints off the dump. Let them have at it. It was sort of like having company.

Smoky drained the last slurry of coffee from his tin cup then stretched his suspenders over his shoulders. He walked across the rubbish to where he thought the strange noise had come from. He squinted, reducing the glare of morning light off the heavy dew covering the dump. He wasn't sure, but he thought he could make out footprints traveling across the surface. He lumbered over to where they appeared to stop.

"It wasn't like that yesterday," he said, noticing a metal chair leg protruding from the trash. "Ellie wouldn't have left that sticking up." He pulled the chair out of the pile, dislodging a box of old medical books Dr. Fichet had dumped on Friday. Smoky had squirreled away one colorful fold-out atlas that contained detailed drawings of female anatomy.

Smoky lifted his cap and scratched the top of his bald head. Something wasn't right. That red blanket wasn't there yesterday either. He would've seen that for sure, would've kept it for next winter's drafts. He took a step forward, grabbed hold of the blanket's tattered edge, and gave it a tug. It was caught on something heavy. Not wanting to tear it, he cleared away a few bags of garbage and a cardboard box holding a handful of spent shotgun shells and a moth-eaten green and black plaid hunting jacket.

The blanket wouldn't budge, so he knelt on his swollen knee, grabbed hold with both hands and pulled hard. He recoiled as a man's arm fell out of the blanket like a dead fish out of wrapping paper, its bluish hand settling onto a dew-soaked pile of disintegrating funny pages.

"Where'd *you* come from?" Smoky lifted the blanket, saw the back of the man's head, scraggly white hair rimming a threadbare collar. "Never seen a dead guy in *my* dump." An uncomfortable shiver went clear through him. He looked around, felt like he was doing something wrong and was about to get caught.

"'Spose I should call the sheriff. Have his boys come down, investigate."

He looked at the body again. There was something familiar about the man's overcoat and sausage-like fingers. Smoky straightened up, checked the front gate, which was locked tight with a logging chain and padlock. It was Sunday. No one should be coming. He looked at the dead man again. "Might as well see who you are," he said out loud, as if deputies were listening at the edge of the woods. "Sheriff will ask me, anyway." He lowered his voice. "Not that I owe the damn sheriff anything."

Smoky had rolled over dead soldiers in the war, had seen men's *last stares* before. It was always haunting, but after all, he was responsible for what went on at the dump. He reached over and rolled the stiff body toward him, revealing an empty whiskey bottle and a third arm, a woman's arm, under the man, under the red blanket. It looked as though they had died embracing each other. Smoky slowly turned the man's face toward the sunrise.

"Freddie!" he said, startled. "Not you, Freddie Knapp."

Smoky recognized a butterfly tattoo on the back of the woman's hand. Smoky pushed the dirty blanket away from her face. His shoulders sank. "Rose—" He shook his head. "Freddie and Rose. What the hell happened? You piss somebody off?"

Smoky looked them over. Not a bruise or spot of blood anywhere. He pulled the blanket back farther, revealing another empty fifth of cheap gin and a spent bottle of pain pills.

"Ah, Freddie, I knew things got bad. Cancer, they said. Lotta' pain. Heard they wanted to put you in a nursing home. Well, good for you, old buddy, you didn't let them."

Freddie's and Rose's eyes were closed. There was no *last stare*. Smoky tucked the blanket under their heads, making them look more comfortable. "The two of you always said you'd go out together." He looked at Freddie. "And you promised you'd come back to the farm someday, and here you are." He noticed the irregular scar on Freddie's cheek where the barbed fishing hook tore through one afternoon on the Moose River the spring they quit high school. Smoky reached down, touched his friend's cold skin. "I'd been meaning to come by, but I don't venture too far since I lost my license that last time. They let me drive Ellie inside the dump is all."

Smoky stood, righted the metal chair, and sat down. Hi lifted the oily brim of his cap and scratched the top of his head. "Boy, we had some fun when we was kids. Fishing together on Joe's Pond, jumping off cliffs up to Willoughby Lake." Smoky smiled. "My favorite was chasin' coons through cornfields in Peacham in the middle of the night with kerosene lanterns. And deer camp at Uncle Pete's shack in Newark. You and I stealing licks off Canadian whisky bottles while the men smoked cigars and played poker most of the night."

Smoky switched his toothpick to the other side of his mouth. "I probably never told you, but I felt bad about you and your brother losin' this place after your folks died. The town could have helped you keep farming, helped develop the sugar woods on the north ridge. Would've produced enough to keep you out of hock." Smoky shook his head. "It was a raw deal. Town needed a good place for a dump is all."

Smoky leaned forward and tried to straighten Freddy's overcoat. "I know you was upset when the town hired me to take care of this place, but Sis was sick and I needed work bad after the trucking company let me go." He looked down toward the river's edge. "I've taken good care of your old swimming hole; kept the trash away from the bank."

Smoky looked at Rose, lifted a curl of matted gray hair out of her eyes. "Rosey, you were always my beauty. Even though you run off with this old coot, I never gave up on you. Never forgot that kiss behind the hay wagon on the Fourth of July."

Smoky stood and addressed his friends. "I suppose you want me to take care of business or you wouldn't have crawled in here and drunk yourselves to death." He checked the gate again. "Tell you what, I'll fire up Ellie and we'll get you buried down by the river. You don't need no official burying. Screw the sheriff. Law's nothing but trouble."

Smoky covered Freddie and Rose with the blanket and walked back to the *Cat House.* Inside he stared at his work bench, piled high with tobacco cans overflowing with spark plugs, spare carburetor parts, screws, nails, and rusted bolts of every variety. On a shelf above the bench sat a collection of rescued appliances including a chrome toaster and a coffee percolator that actually worked. Above the shelf hung the lucky bamboo fishing pole he'd won from Freddie playing poker when they were teenagers. Its line unkempt and sagging, he hadn't fished with it in decades, but he'd always kept it nearby.

Smoky kicked a couple of liquor bottles out of the way and climbed up onto a chair. Steadying himself against the wall, he reached as high as he could and took down the dusty pole. The cork handle still had a good feel to it. He slid the pole into Ellie's cab then walked over to the windowsill where he kept a sap bucket full of artificial flowers people had thrown away over the years. He pulled out several of the least faded red and white roses, wiped the cobwebs off then jammed them into his pocket and climbed up into the seat.

Smoky touched two bare wires together under the dash. Sparks snapped then the engine growled to life, quickly enveloping the ceiling with blue diesel smoke. He raised the bucket and backed out into the yard. A breeze had kicked up, carrying heavy clouds up the river valley from the south. He glanced at the front gate then drove across the expanse of rubbish to the red blanket, the familiar clanking of Ellie's steel track a comfort to him. He lowered the bucket in front of Freddie and Rose, shut off the engine, and climbed down.

The inside of the steel bucket was rusted and stained with a pallet of eggshells, oil and grease, old paint and roofing tar. Smoky looked around, retrieved a box of newspapers that looked fairly dry, and spread them along the bottom of the bucket. He leaned down and pulled back the blanket. "Okay, folks, may be a bit of a rough ride, but I'm going to get you buried proper."

He dragged their bodies up onto the lip of the bucket, then climbed inside and pulled and tugged till they were well onto the newspapers. "Heavier 'n I thought," he said, resting for a moment.

As he climbed out of the bucket, he heard a loud yell then the rattle of chains at the front gate. He peered around Ellie. "Shit—"

"Smokeee! Get over here and open this gate."

Smoky's heart raced. It was that asshole, Chuck Amidon, from the selectboard, a deputy sheriff to boot. Probably needed to dump some stuff he didn't want his old lady to see.

"Hurry up!" Amidon yelled, dropping the tailgate of his pickup.

Smoky walked as fast as he could, his breathing having a hard time keeping up with him. By the time he got to the gate, Amidon was sucking on a cigarette,

impatiently gesturing toward Ellie. Smoky reached into his pocket for the padlock key.

"Bring that machine of yours over here," Amidon said, flicking his cigarette
into the dirt.

"Stalled out. Won't start," Smoky said, pushing the key into the lock.

"Then just get this stuff unloaded. I got to get back to town."

"Ain't supposed to open the dump on Sundays," Smoky said, as he pulled the
chain through the steel gate.

"Do what I say, Latrell. Don't forget I can kick your ass out of here
anytime." Amidon looked at Smoky and smirked. "No one else would hire
a crazy old drunk who walks around with plastic flowers hanging out of his
overalls?"

Smoky felt cold sweat forming on the nape of his neck. He'd forgotten about
the flowers. He pulled one side of the gate open. "Just dump it here. I'll move
it later."

"Open the damn gate and I'll back over to the pile."

It would be too close. Amidon might see where Smoky'd dragged Freddie
and Rose out of the trash.

"Leave it here. I'll push it over later when I get the dozer going." Smoky
stared at the ground.

"Oh, what the hell. Just hurry up."

Smoky started pulling boxes of beer bottles and girlie magazines off the
truck. Amidon lit another smoke while he stood there watching him. "You're
acting even weirder than usual, Latrell."

Smoky ignored him and finished unloading. Amidon climbed into his pickup, flicked his cigarette out the window and drove off, spraying gravel behind
him.

"Asshole," Smoky said. "With guys like that running the town, I'm glad I
live out here." He picked up the logging chain, ran it through the steel gates and
padlocked them together again.

After he was sure Amidon was gone, Smoky walked back to Ellie and
leaned against her heavy steel track to rest. He wondered if he was about to do
something sacrilegious. Wondered if he needed to go find a minister, somebody

official. He looked at his friends lying together in the bucket. "Ah, what the hell—" he said. He'd been to funerals over the years and guessed he could say a few words before he put them in the ground.

He climbed up into the cab, brought the bucket off the ground, and headed down toward the river. Clouds made their way up the valley like a slow moving train, their undersides illuminated with a pale red glow.

A hundred yards or so below the dump, he stopped Ellie on a level grassy area just above a bend in the river. He lowered the bucket and stared down at the murky spring current swirling around tree limbs and old tires caught along the bank. Then he looked at his dead friends. At that moment it seemed life had gone by too fast, though at other times it sure had seemed to drag.

Smoky climbed down off Ellie, pulled a long-handled shovel from the back. He found a soft spot in the ground and cut out a good sized section. He rolled back the sod and began removing the loam and underlying gravel a shovelful at a time. It wasn't long before his back and shoulders started aching. Usually he had a few pops in him by this hour but, strangely, he didn't feel like drinking. He rested for a few minutes, checked on his friends then commenced digging again.

By noontime, the hole was a good two feet down, deep enough to keep the animals from digging them up. He was anxious to get them in the ground before anyone caught him, but felt himself hesitating, wanting to keep Freddie and Rose on the green side of the turf a little longer.

Suddenly, he heard a shot in the distance across the river. Probably some kid out rabbit hunting with a .22. Smoky drove the shovel into the pile of dirt and walked over to Ellie. "It's time," he said, nodding to his friends. He'd angled the bucket so they would slide out easier than they went in. He grabbed hold of the blanket and pulled hard. Freddie and Rose slid over the steel lip of the bucket onto the wet ground at the edge of the grave, which gave way beneath his and their weight. Smoky lost his footing and, still holding onto the blanket, fell backwards into the hole, Freddie and Rose almost landing on top of him. As their bodies settled on the bottom, he quickly pushed himself back against the earthen side wall.

"Not enough room for all of us." He reached over, covered their faces with the edge of the blanket then scrambled out of the grave on all fours. He stood at the edge of the hole, gave them one more look. "Sorry, folks, I ain't going with you."

Smoky walked over, pulled the fishing pole and the flowers out of the cab. He laid the pole alongside Freddie. It took a minute or so to throw in the first shovelful of dirt, but then he quickly covered them with a good thick layer. He used Ellie to push the rest of the dirt back into the hole then flattened it out. He rolled the sod over the topsoil and tamped the edges with his boots.

When he was done, he stepped back, pulled the flowers from his pocket, and pushed them into the grass above his friends' heads. All in all, he thought it looked pretty good. Peaceful there by the river.

Smoky tried to think of a few words to say. He knew preachers always said something about ashes and dust, but he was real tired. His body ached awful, and he really needed a drink.

He turned away and climbed up into Ellie's familiar seat. For a few moments he looked at the subtle depression in the ground. "You'll be all right now," he said, nodding. He backed Ellie around and headed for home.

Chapter 3

No Sharks in Vermont

Growing up, Grandpa Joe was my hero. My mother had hemorrhaged badly during my delivery and wasn't strong enough to take care of me. My father, a restless railroad man, left town for good the night I was born. So my life began as an only child on our small family farm on the Canadian border, held together by the strength of my maternal grandparents. Sadly, Grandma died when I was six. Mother passed the day after I turned eight.

Grandpa Joe, however, was always there for me. He taught me how to drive a tractor and then a pickup as soon as my feet could reach the pedals. He trained me how to gently wash a cow's teats and how to plane a spruce plank to within a cat's whisker of square. He showed me how to harvest corn just before the coons stole it and how to silently track a buck by the light of a November moon.

I was seven the first time Grandpa took me fishing out on the "Big Lake." On that cool May morning, a thin layer of fog hovered over the dark surface of Lake Champlain, the four hundred foot deep glacial remnant of the great inland sea between the Adirondacks of New York and the Green Mountains of Vermont. Before that I'd fished small streams and rivers with him but hadn't been old enough to go out on Champlain. I felt small sitting in that little aluminum boat trying to comprehend the vast body of water stretched out before us. I must have looked apprehensive because Grandpa turned to me, patted me on the knee and said, "Don't worry, Nicholas, no sharks in these waters, not anywhere in Vermont." Though the thought had never crossed my mind, I felt oddly relieved.

Grandpa tied me into a life jacket that had pockets in front filled with lead sinkers and little red and white plastic bobbers. He laid his silver thermos of chocolate-flavored coffee on the floor next to the red gas tank and sat me in the bow as a counterweight to him and the outboard motor. He pulled hard on the ten-horse Evinrude and it sputtered to life. We pushed off from the wooden dock and headed north through the cool mist toward his favorite fishing spot near Shepherd's Island, the northern tip of which lay just over the Canadian border.

The February before I finished medical training in New York, my girl-friend, Isabella, broke up with me, refusing to move to Vermont where I had committed to practice. I thought a fishing trip to Mexico would do me good, so I called Grandpa Joe and asked him to go with me. At first he was hesitant. He'd only been out of Vermont twice: once on a three-year tour of duty in the army during World War II, the other when he took Grandma on their honey-moon to the "amazing" Iowa State Fair. After a little convincing, however, he decided it would be fun to go south of the border, a grand adventure before he turned eighty.

As we approached Hathaway Point heading to the broad lake, Grandpa slowed the motor, reached for his coffee and took a long swig. Choppy water waited for us beyond the point. "Have some before it gets cold." He handed me the thermos. The rich, chocolate mix-ture burned my tongue, but I swallowed it, then turned away and quickly drew in a breath of cool, moist air. He revved the engine and we headed out onto the lake.

Grandpa Joe and I enjoyed a relaxed few days on a charter boat, the blis-tering Mexican sun searing my neck and shoulders. After fishing all morning off the coast of Isla Mujeres, our local guide, Rafael, had taken us snorkeling over an ancient reef a mile off shore. I was tired and glad to be resting back in the boat. Grandpa Joe, fascinated by a pair of brilliant yellow, green and blue parrot fish – like nothing he'd ever seen before – was still snorkeling fifty feet away.

Crossing the heavy chop of the broad lake I suddenly felt queasy and almost threw up. Holding tight to the gunwale, I steadied myself as I watched Grandpa's strong, outstretched arm steer the motor. He didn't take his hand off the throttle until we reached his special spot over a thick green weed bed stretching along the west side of the island. Our lines in the water, he seemed delighted when my rod was the first to dip. "You've got one," he said, sliding closer to me on the seat. "That's it. Now reel him in."

Rafael handed me a sweaty bottle of water from the cooler. I drank most of it then poured the rest over my sunburned face. As I sat there in the boat, I wondered if Joe—despite his stubborn insistence— should be out there snorkeling alone.

I cranked hard on my Sears and Roebuck reel as Grandpa leaned over the side and helped me land a fat sunfish, which flopped around in the bottom of the boat, its shiny tail slapping against the aluminum. He grabbed the slimy catch with one hand, flicked the hook out of its gaping mouth, and handed the fish to me. I admired it for a few moments then threw it back into the lake. We didn't eat sunfish.

Rafael pointed to a subtle ripple on the surface of the ocean, a small rogue wave not following the others.

An avid hunter and farmyard butcher, Grandpa was completely at ease with killing things. Swiftly. Efficiently. He not only slaughtered his own pigs, cows and chickens, he butchered for other farmers as well. Sometimes I'd go with him in his International truck set up with a winch, hoist, a chest of knives, ropes and cleavers, and a deep-bottomed iron kettle to hold the fiercely boiling water into which he'd dip headless chickens before he plucked them clean enough you'd think they'd been struck by lightning.

There was a sudden change in Joe's countenance. He lifted his mask onto his forehead and remained motionless in the water. He scanned the horizon as I'd seen him do many times hunting in the deep north woods. Rafael reached for a pole spear hooked to the side of the boat.

When Grandpa was butchering, I'd stand mesmerized at the emotionless efficiency of his craft, trying not to stare at the mounting pile of dying yellow and red chicken heads. Occasionally he'd pause with a hen, a turkey, or the hind leg of a pig caught in his large hand and notice the uneasy look on my face. He'd cock his head a bit and say, "Somebody's got to do it, might as well be me. Kill 'em quick, that's the thing." Then he'd land another clean blow with his cleaver on the chopping block. "Never let 'em suffer."

I didn't see the shark on his first strike. It didn't even show its dorsal fin; there was only an effervescent swirling on the surface of the water where the shiny gray predator made his approach. He hit the underside of our wooden boat with a jarring thud. Joe was a good stone's throw away, floating alone over a reef of delicate white coral.

The perch were plentiful that day and we filled our buckets by noon, at which point Grandpa dropped anchor just off the weed bed so we could have lunch. The Canadian bacon and cheddar cheese sandwiches tasted great to me, though he said they weren't as good as Grandma's used to be. She'd drowned the year before hurrying home during a spring flood, an old bridge suddenly collapsing beneath her Oldsmobile. Her death sorely tested my grandfather's temper and his faith. I think he would have fired his .30-.30 into the sky and shook his fists at God in heaven except he knew Grandma was up there.

"Shark!" Rafael yelled, crouching below the gunwale of the boat. I glanced over the side. The surface of the water was eerily calm, though the size of Rafael's eyes spoke to the danger.

"Get down—" Rafael commanded in a hushed, urgent tone.

I think my underlying dread began around the time Grandma died in that flood, but it became palpable the Easter weekend two years later when Mother died. Wracked with pneumonia, she succumbed on the sparsely furnished ward of the county hospital. Without a word, she took her last breath, a sigh really, like she'd finally crossed the finish line after a long, agonizing race.

On the way home from the cemetery, I figured I'd spend the rest of my life with Grandpa on our hillside farm. As much as I revered my grandfather, that realization somehow frightened me. He and I were such different people. He had a peace about him, walking through life with faith the good earth would always produce another harvest, the forests another load of fresh timber. He didn't complain about life's unpredictability, never seemed to want for anything. He believed God would give him the strength and guidance to get through each day till He was done with him.

I loved my home in the foothills of the Green Mountains, but I grew up with a smoldering fear that permeated this land of rugged beauty. I did have three good friends, two of which were the Cory brothers, our neighbors a half mile up the road. On summer weekends we'd fish and float down the Missisquoi River on old inner tubes, and occasionally, Grandpa took us to the dump with our .22s where we'd plink bottles and shoot rats until the crazy old dump keep, Smokey Latrell, stumbled out of his shed and ran us off.

My other friend was Doc Parsons, who was especially kind to me during my mother's last months. He kept me busy with odd jobs in his office: filing charts, cleaning exam rooms and sterilizing his surgical instruments. During down time, I'd thumb through anatomy and surgery books in his study. That's where I developed a fascination with medicine that eventually led me to medical school in New York.

I saw Joe silently treading water, gradually closing the distance between himself and our boat. Rafael remained crouched, his large, bloodshot eyes darting back and forth. "Come!" he called, waving Joe toward us. I started the outboard and pointed the bow toward him. "Easy," Rafael said.

Heading home that afternoon, Lake Champlain was calm, warm sunshine accompanying us back into the bay. After we rounded a large rock outcropping covered with land-locked seagulls, Grandpa cut the Evinrude and popped the top on the one bottle of Narragansett beer he allowed himself after fishing. "These are good days, Nicholas," he said, smiling. "They make life tolerable." I nodded in agreement.

My grandfather was part of the town's backbone. A fair man, he owned two farms and the local lumber mill that together employed almost a hundred people in a town of well less than a thousand. He didn't suffer lazy men well, but if a man was honest and worked hard, Grandpa did anything he could to help him. He could have been a rich man if he'd wanted, but Grandpa was far more interested in spending his money to better the community. People appreciated that he built a new baseball diamond on one of his fields, and outfitted an automotive shop behind the mill so his men could repair and customize their own rigs at minimal cost. And for as long as I could remember, he paid for the town's annual chicken barbecue and fireworks display on the Fourth of July.

Joe was less than twenty feet from the boat when the shiny triangular fin sliced through the water in front of us. He froze, only his eyes following the movement of the shark. "Rafael," I whispered, "throw him the rope." Rafael motioned for me to be still. As the fin disappeared beneath the surface again, Joe continued swimming, edging closer to the boat. When he was just a few yards away, Rafael and I leaned far over the gunwale, stretching our arms toward him.

Back at the dock, Grandpa winched the boat onto its trailer then drove his pickup to a campsite at water's edge. I helped him build a fire in a stone pit among cedars that hung low over the lake. He slid his filet knife between the delicate bones and meat of half a bucket of perch then handed me the filets so I could dunk them in the paper bag containing his special mixture of cornmeal, minced onions, herbs, and finely ground sea salt.

I loved the aroma of seasoned perch sizzling over an open fire and never ceased to be amazed at the number Grandpa could eat. Afterwards, he'd invariably relax against a log and reminisce about running the Germans out of Bayeux, France after D-Day. I noticed, however, that he never spoke of what actually happened when they landed on Omaha Beach until one day out fishing I asked him about it directly. He thought about it for a few moments then offered only that it was a "hard landing," and that 'the boys who made it over the bluffs fought with determination God had never seen before." I never asked about his war experience again.

I stretched my hand toward Joe as far as I could, the boat nearly capsizing under my weight. His fingers reached for mine as a violent surge of water came up from beneath him. Fleeting relief turned to horror as Joe's fingers slipped from mine. Despite the near hundred degree temperature, an icy sweat broke over my neck and back. Joe's eyes suddenly snapped wide open—like he'd been shot—his rigid body jolting backwards. An awful purple-red swirl appeared in the blue water.

When we finished eating, Grandpa dumped the fish heads and bones at the edge of the woods then we knelt along the shoreline and washed our hands in the cold lake.

Rafael lunged and grabbed my leg, preventing me from going overboard. I yelled to Joe as his body jerked violently back and forth then raced away from us, his torso pushed through the water like the figurehead on the prow of a sinking ship.

Suddenly, Joe raised both hands in the air and let out a roar, like the time he got between a bear cub and its mother and had to face her down. His powerful fists rained down on the forehead of the shark, which turned sharply back toward our boat. As they raced toward us, Joe's body weakened, his head falling to the side, his arms sinking into the water.

As the shark rammed Joe into our boat, I reached out and grabbed his shoulder but couldn't hold on. I drew my diving knife from its sheath, raised it over my head and waited for the fish to come around again, now much of my grandfather a grizzly red trail behind the shark.

"Kill 'em quick, that's the thing. Never let 'em suffer."

As the shark made one last pass, I lunged toward it, slashing across its forehead with my knife. The shark stopped swimming. Its jaw jerked, relaxing its grip on my grandfather's torso. As I raised my knife again, Joe's lifeless body turned. I caught a glimpse of his glazed-over eyes. In that strange, poignant moment I knew he wouldn't want me to kill the great fish, even if I could. I hesitated for a split second, my mind's eye flashing with images of Joe standing among piles of chicken and turkey heads, boiling black cauldrons, and freshly plucked feathers carried on the wind. I saw the desperate looks on lake trout, perch, and bass lying in the bottom of our little boat.

As the images cleared, I realized the shark had disappeared into the sea. I searched the water trying to find my grandfather, but he was gone. Like Joe, the shark, in its own way, had been merciful.

I felt a sense of peace riding back to the farm in Grandpa's pickup. He seemed happiest when returning from a fishing trip, his belly full of perch and his one beer. A checkered wool blanket covered the pickup's seat and I appreciated that he always let me sit behind the stick shift next to him. As darkness fell, our warm yellow headlamps illuminated the dirt road ahead of us as we drove through Folsom's Hollow toward home.

Rafael and I drifted in stunned silence, staring at a calmed sea. Before long, Joe's remains surfaced. His eyes were closed and what was left of his body was pale. I knew my medical training was as useless as my despair. Rafael took hold of one of Joe's arms and we pulled him over the side into the bottom of the boat. Rafael threw a fishing net—which was all he had—over the lower half of Joe's torso. It looked like we'd harvested him from the sea.

"So sorry," he said to me in broken English. Tears welled from behind the terror in his eyes. "Never had man killed," he said, staring at Joe. He made the sign of the cross several times, reciting something in Spanish I'm sure was a prayer.

When we arrived back at the farm, I ran upstairs to my mother's room at the end of the hall. Her bed was positioned so she could see out the dormer window that overlooked our backyard collection of disabled farm machinery and rusting cars.

Mother's door was always closed. I paused and listened before I turned the doorknob and stepped inside. She was so thin that with the disheveled covers over her it was hard to tell if she was really there. I carefully lifted the comforter and saw her sleeping, her once dark and silky hair turned to a scraggly yellow-gray. I gently stroked it. Her hair didn't hurt like the rest of her.

She awakened when I sat on the edge of her bed. Managing a vacant smile, she reached up and touched my cheek with bony fingers that then fell back into her ever-shrinking world of rumpled sheets, dusty curtains and house flies floating in half-emptied water glasses.

When Rafael landed on the white sand of Isla Mujeres, other fisherman ran to help pull our boat onto the beach. When they saw my grandfather's body, they froze, sharing looks of shock and horror. I knew from their faces that a tourist, particularly an *American* tourist, had never been killed on one of their fishing trips. I sat there, sunburned and sick, Grandpa Joe cradled in a salt-encrusted fishing net at my feet.

A part of me wanted to tell Rafael and his friends that things would be okay, that it was no one's fault. That this time Joe was bettered by a fish hungrier than he was. But I was too exhausted to speak. Two villagers in brightly colored shorts helped me out of the boat. My temples pounded. Dizzy and disoriented, I fell to the wet sand and wretched violently, warm salt water lapping at my knees.

The men carefully carried Joe's body to a thatch-roofed cabana just off the beach. They laid him on a bed of palm leaves spread out on the ground, treating him with the respect and care shown a fallen elder.

Even out of the direct sun, it was oppressively hot. My body was sunburned and sweaty. A young boy handed me a cold bottle of water. I took it and sort of collapsed in a corner, where I started to cry. I wanted to feel the cool mountain air of home, for all of this to be a nightmare. I wanted Isabella to hold me tight against her.

Soon an old man with long white hair—a priest of sorts—arrived, and the other villagers stepped outside. The man bowed his head and prayed over my grandfather. Then he took my arm, helped me up, and walked me over to Joe. We knelt together in front of the body. The man spoke in Spanish, passing his hand over Joe's face, which looked strangely peaceful there on the green palm leaves. I didn't understand what he was saying, but I knew it was a blessing for Joe, for me, and for his village.

After a few minutes, the man stood and motioned for me to stay. He walked out of the cabana, the white cloth door closing behind him. Kneeling in front of Joe, I knew it was time to say good-bye. I took hold of his stiff hand, and intertwined his strong fingers with mine. My chin began to quiver. Through tears and briny sweat I looked into his face. "You gave me everything good in my life," I whispered. "You know how much I loved you."

When the cool darkness finally came, I slept on a woven blanket next to my grandfather. I was aware of Rafael and other villagers outside around a campfire, and was appreciative that they kept checking on me during the night.

The next day I flew back from Cancun with Grandpa Joe riding beneath me in the cargo hold of the plane. That first night home was the loneliest I'd ever been. I stood in our eerily quiet farmhouse staring at Joe's barn coat hanging on the back of the kitchen door. After a while, I took it down and slid my arms into its softened sleeves. I drifted around the house, feeling his presence everywhere. I picked up his worn leather gloves and smelled the mixture of pine pitch and motor oil. I appreciated the familiar mustiness emanating from the dirt basement where he kept racks of canned tomatoes, corn, beans, beets, pickled cow's tongue and pig's feet. I remembered the sweet smell of moist wool from his boot socks, now long dry, hanging on a sash cord strung across the south bay window above the Christmas cactus he'd kept alive for twenty-odd years since my grandmother died.

I climbed the staircase and listened at Mother's old door then pushed it open. My faded first grade picture, cockeyed in its frame, still stood on her bureau.

I remembered the morning I sat on the end of my mother's bed and told her that I was going to go to college. She smiled. Years later I decided to become a physician and return home to fill the void left after Doc Parsons died. They'd been unable to attract another doctor to settle in our small town, so his office, though outdated, was still waiting for me. It was just the way he left it the night he slumped over a pile of patient charts, dead of a heart attack at age seventy-four.

I had been conflicted when I left for college, feeling guilty I wasn't home working on the farm and taking charge of Grandpa's saw mill. When

I occasionally got a weekend off, I drove back from New York. I loved those visits, but it wasn't the same as beginning each day doing chores with Grandpa, sharing homemade donuts and coffee in the milking parlor as the sun climbed over the Cold Hollow Mountains.

After a few hours of sleep, I rose to a red sky, got dressed and walked outside. It had stormed overnight, topping the tractors and junk cars with pure white snow. Despite my plans to move home, I had a strong feeling this might be the last time I'd see the farm. I made my way through snow drifts to Joe's tool shed. I took a claw hammer off the bench and walked over to a black Plymouth four-door sitting in a thatch work of frozen hay beside the barn. This was Gram and Grandpa's first car, bought with his army discharge pay when he came home from the war. It was behind the Plymouth's steering wheel that I first learned to drive. I must have cruised a thousand miles while Grandpa Joe led heifers back and forth between the pasture and the milking parlor.

Much as I hated to disturb its original appearance, I had to take a piece of the old girl with me. I brushed snow off the front of the hood revealing the chrome grill which was pitted with rust. Feeling a bit sacrilegious, I slid the hammer's claw beneath the chrome and carefully jimmied it loose. All but one rivet pulled through the decaying supports. The last bolt held on as I twisted it back and forth several times. I hit it with the hammer, but it would not let go. Cold and frustrated, I walked over to Joe's International and retrieved a large meat cleaver from the butchering chest in the back. With one fell swoop, I severed the stubborn bolt, the chrome face of the Plymouth falling into the snow at my feet.

I called and arranged a meeting with Charles Hayden, Joe's attorney. Charles was a prickly sort of fellow, short of stature, long on ego. He explained Joe's estate, which consisted of the lumber mill and the thousand or so acres of prime timberland surrounding it, our home farm, and the old Gregory place Joe had bought for its hay fields back in the sixties. He had left everything to me.

When Mr. Hayden finished reviewing the will, he looked over his bifocals. "Seeing as you're opening your medical office next summer, we need a plan for the properties between now and then. Your grandfather wouldn't want things falling into disrepair. That's when vandals take over."

I closed my eyes and remembered standing in line to order my favorite pastrami on rye sandwich at Zabar's Deli in Manhattan, my head filled with the aromas of a dozen gourmet coffees lined up in gleaming silver vessels along the counter. I saw Isabella sitting across from me at dinner in the Village, candle-light illuminating her smooth olive skin. I thought of the painful moment I told her I was moving back to Vermont. She'd lowered her head, long black hair falling over her shoulders. "You'll have to go without me," she had said in her soft, raspy voice. Then she looked at me through squinted eyes. "I love you, Nicholas, but I can't leave the City."

After that night the closeness we had shared during our three years together shifted and began slipping away. We were in love but just as she couldn't leave her home in New York, I couldn't abandon Joe in Vermont. Spending nights alone for the first time in years was hard. I was lonely and I thought a fishing trip with Joe would solidify my wavering frame of mind on moving back to the Green Mountain State.

I realized Mr. Hayden was still sitting at his desk, staring at me. "I'll call you this afternoon with instructions," I said.

He seemed surprised, offended even, that I didn't want more of his advice. He stood and took a step around his desk. "Don't you want to review the books of the mill operation and the farms?" He took off his wire-rimmed glasses and set them, rather dramatically, on his mahogany desk.

I stood. "I'll call you this afternoon."

"I know your grandfather would want—"

"Mr. Hayden," I said with uncharacteristic sternness, "I know what my grandfather would want."

I walked out of his office into the cold February air, climbed into Joe's pickup and drove back to the farm.

It was ten degrees and snowing hard the morning of the service. I walked up the scalloped granite steps of the Methodist Church clear in my love for my grand-father but uncertain of what I would say when the minister asked me to speak.

I sat quietly in the second pew in front of Joe's simple wood coffin, waiting as the church filled with his townspeople. A few rows behind me, the postmaster,

Fred Sherman, sat with his wife, Edith. He had criticized me for going off to college and not taking over the farm as Joe had wanted. And I'd heard he was furious I'd taken Joe way down to Mexico fishing.

Charlotte Fitch, from the drug store, sat to my right, her white-gloved hands in her lap gripping a handkerchief. She'd long had an unrequited soft spot for Joe. Behind her sat our old neighbors, the Cory boys, whom I hadn't seen since I left for college.

I was startled when Miss Daniels, the eighty-two year old organist, struck up a slow rendition of "The Battle Hymn of the Republic." When she finished, Reverend Cummings rose from his chair to the wooden pulpit and slid on his glasses. He adjusted the purple velvet marker splitting a gold-edged Bible then looked across the congregation.

"It is both hard and an honor to preside over this service for a man I have been friends with since we learned to fish together in grammar school. I feel comforted, however, by the presence of so many good friends. Though we want to celebrate Joe's remarkably good life, we must also acknowledge and embrace the sadness we feel in our hearts. We can put on our best funeral faces, but we must be honest in the presence of God."

Several women began to softly weep. I wanted the reverend to get on with it.

"Would the congregation please rise for our opening hymn?"

Some of the older folks were slow pushing up from their pews. When everyone was standing, Miss Daniels led the congregation through three plodding verses of "How Great Thou Art" then we all sat back down.

Somewhere during a scripture reading from Mark or John, I lost concentration, hearing only the familiar echo of voices in the church I'd attended as a child. I didn't fully come back to the service until I realized Reverend Cummings had just introduced me as "Joe's beloved grandson" and that he was motioning me forward.

I stood, straightened my suit coat and stepped to the pulpit. I felt embraced by the church, filled with everyone's love for Joe, even though I knew there was some resentment toward me. Farmers stood in the back in their work overalls, hats under their arms. The American Legion honor guard stood at the sides of the church and four generations of McClowskys sat close together in the pew their family had occupied for over a century. Mrs. Calbeck, widow of Joe's longtime lumber foreman, sat with her grandkids on both sides of her. At the rear door stood a tired Clyde Demers with the other red-faced men of the town road crew. After plowing all night through the storm, they stood solemnly in the shadow of the balcony, their diesel trucks idling outside.

The silence in the church caught me off guard. I cleared my throat. "I haven't known exactly what I'd say today. I guess I still can't quite believe my grandfather's dead. I've kept hoping I'd wake up from this nightmare, but seeing all of you here today helps make it more real, and somehow, more tolerable. Your abiding love for Joe is a comfort."

I steadied both hands on the edges of the lectern. "I want to share a few things I think Joe would want me to say. Despite the violence of his death, I know when he died my grandfather was at peace with his life and with his God. He was a brave man who, I believe, understood and accepted that it was his time."

I tasted blood-stained sea water and felt the merciless Mexican sun beating down on my neck. I struggled to keep my composure.

"I want you to know how much Joe cared for this town and for all of you. He would want you to know that he left the entire mill operation to the men who work there." I nodded at the faces of the mill men scattered throughout the congregation. "The Missisquoi Lumber Mill now belongs to you."

A murmur went through the congregation. Attorney Hayden's eyes opened wide. The faces of mill families looked shocked, tears appearing in some of their eyes.

Trying to keep my chin from quivering, I continued. "I want you to know how deeply I loved my grandfather. He was an exceptionally strong, kind man. He literally steered me through my life to this point."

I paused and caught my breath.

"I'm not sure what we'll all do without Joe to guide us, but in the quiet moments since I arrived back in town I've had to come to grips with something that has dogged me my whole life. Since my mother died, I have lived in terrible fear of losing Joe. Now that he's gone, I realize that it was him, his presence in my life, that made me want to come back to practice medicine here."

The church was so quiet I could hear the hissing of air brakes on the plow trucks out front.

"As beautiful as this place is, as good as you people are, this is no longer my home. For me it is a solemn place where I have lost, one by one, all the family I ever had." I took in a deep breath. "I've decided I won't be moving back to practice in Doc Parson's office."

There was a collective catching of breath in the congregation, bodies stiffening in the pews, as if I'd just endorsed the Yankees against the Red Sox in the last game of the pennant race.

"God bless you all," I said quietly.

I stepped back from the lectern. Reverend Cummings, who also looked surprised, shook my hand then I walked back to my pew.

The reverend closed with words of thanksgiving and redemption, followed by the congregation reciting the Lord's Prayer. Miss Daniels accompanied our filing out of the church with a mournful rendition of "Faith of Our Fathers," the same hymn she had played at the end of Gram's service twenty years before. I still remembered Grandpa Joe's strong arms holding me that day.

Looking straight ahead, I walked down the church steps, through the snow to my car. I slid into the driver's seat and gripped the leather-covered steering wheel. The town trucks led the procession to the cemetery on the outskirts of town. I followed behind Mr. Martin's black Cadillac hearse as cold Canadian winds whipped gusts of snow across the road, pushing hard against the side of my BMW. As the long line of vehicles rolled through the familiar white countryside, images of Grandpa Joe, old and new, passed through my exhausted mind.

A deputy sheriff directed traffic at the entrance to the cemetery. When it was my turn to pull off the highway, I closed my eyes and saw Joe's steady arm piloting his outboard through choppy water that foggy morning out on the Big Lake.

I swerved around the deputy and headed into the storm toward New York. Despite the treacherous patches of black ice and the driving snow in my headlights, I pushed the gas pedal harder to the floor. I couldn't get away from home fast enough.

Chapter 4

End of the Season

With his good shoulder, Harlan pushed the shed door closed against a cold Canadian wind and slid a load of fresh-split kindling off his arm into the wood box. He hung his coat on the rocker in front of the stove and straightened his back. The aroma of baby powder and urine drifted into the kitchen from the living room where Martha lay on the electric hospital bed he'd rented when she'd lost her right leg to a lack of circulation and could no longer climb the stairs. He changed her as often as he could, but trying to keep up with chores, cooking, and housework, he wasn't always fast enough and her bottom got raw. A thin layer of zinc oxide with a dusting of powder usually did the trick.

Harlan rubbed his hands together over the woodstove then took down a diaper from a neat stack on the shelf next to Martha's cookbooks. He kept the medical supplies in the kitchen out of her sight. He walked into the living room, where their Christmas tree still stood at the foot of her bed. She loved to watch the reflections of afternoon sunlight on the tinsel and reminisce about treasured ornaments. Though it was late February, on days when the air was particularly quiet, she mentioned still enjoying the fleeting scent of balsam. He knew it was her last chance to enjoy a Christmas tree, so he planned to go to the woods and cut her another before this one had shed itself down to bare twigs.

Harlan sat beside the bed and pulled back the covers. Martha stirred as he undid the adhesive strips holding a diaper around her hips, hips he'd fallen in love with just before the war. Hips he'd held dancing late into summer nights over the lake at the Bayside Pavilion. Hips he'd caressed and kissed in the shadows of their delicate young love making.

Martha awakened and pushed herself up into a sitting position. "Sorry," she said, looking a bit sheepish. "I didn't make it to the commode."

"That's all right," he said, sliding a fresh pad under her. It had been months since she'd even tried to maneuver onto the bedside commode by herself.

Sunlight streamed through the south window illuminating her face. "What a beautiful day," she said. "The children must be so excited."

Martha had marked her many years of teaching by the rhythm of her students' seasonal emotions. Each spring she had brought her class to the farm for a wildflower hunt, leading them through the woods searching for jack-in-the-pulpits, trilliums, trout lilies, and if they were lucky, a few pink lady slippers hiding deep in the pine forest.

Martha turned to Harlan. "The Bobwhites are playing in the hockey championship tonight."

It amazed him how she sometimes had these lucid intervals. Like she hadn't lost a single brain cell to the Alzheimer's that had crept in three years before.

"How did you know?"

"It was on the radio while you were out back."

"I think we're playing Hinesburg."

"That's not far," she said. "We should go."

Harlan was surprised. "Are you strong enough?"

After her last heart attack, Martha had gradually gotten weaker, no longer able to do much without precipitating an attack of angina.

"Yes. I had a wonderful nap."

Harlan heard the gentle puffing of the oxygen apparatus at the head of her bed. "Been a long time since we've seen the Bobwhites play."

"Let's go," Martha said, her eyes brightening. "I've got slap-shot fever!"

Harlan smiled. He hadn't heard that expression in years. "That's my girl," he said, touching her thin white hair. Tired, but excited, he thought about what needed to be done. "I'll call to see if they've any tickets left."

Martha grinned and lay back against her pillows. "You'll find some."

Harlan walked into the kitchen and put a small pot of coffee on to brew. He sat by the woodstove and telephoned his best friend, Harry Thurber, the town fire chief, whose son was the Bobwhite's hockey coach and grandson one of their star players. Harry was delighted Harlan and Martha thought they could make it to the big game. He said he'd have a couple of firemen meet them at six-thirty at the arena in Hinesburg to help get them to their seats.

Martha rested while Harlan fixed grilled cheese sandwiches. After supper, he connected a full oxygen tank to her wheelchair and laid extra wool blankets inside the seat. He changed her into a double layer of fresh diapers then dressed her in her favorite sweat suit and parka. He feared at any moment she would decide not to go or would forget what they were doing all together, but after supper her energy and enthusiasm rallied even more than before.

Around five-thirty, Harlan parked the pickup as close to the front door as he could and left it running. Back inside, he slid Martha into her wheelchair and wrapped the blankets around her shoulders and remaining leg. He propped the door open with a snow shovel and wheeled her out into the cold night. Supporting her arm and hip, he helped her struggle up onto the seat then laid her oxygen tank on the floor at her feet. He pulled the shovel away from the front door and made sure it was closed tight. He lifted her wheelchair into the back, climbed in, and they drove off.

Harlan held Martha's hand on the seat next him on the way to the game. When they arrived, Mike and Nathan, two young firemen, were waiting for them. The arena was a madhouse as hundreds of fans crammed into the bleachers. It had been years since the two high school hockey rivals had met in the state championship, and they both wanted their hands on the trophy.

The firemen guided Martha and Harlan up a ramp to the handicapped platform, which, at center ice, had a commanding view of the rink.

"You've got the best seats in the house," Nathan said, locking Martha's chair in place.

"Thank you, boys," she said, watching the players warming up on the ice.

"This was awfully nice of you, fellas," Harlan said. He sat on a folding chair beside Martha.

"Glad to do it." Mike motioned toward a section of bleachers below them. "We'll be sitting right down there if you need anything."

Both teams played a clean, hard-hitting game. At the end of the second period the score was tied two to two. When the Zamboni came out to resurface the ice, Harlan noticed Martha's breathing was becoming more labored. "You look cold," he said. "Should we go home?"

She smiled. "Not on your life."

He gently rubbed her shoulders and arms with his hands, tucked the woolen blankets in around her, and checked the oxygen tank. "I've got to go to the men's room. I'll be right back."

Harlan made his way through the crowd to the restroom, where it seemed to take forever to relieve himself. He worried about leaving Martha, but he couldn't help it. While everything else seemed to be shrinking, his prostate just kept getting larger.

On the way back to his seat, Harlan paused. Martha looked so small, huddled under the blankets in her wheelchair. It was hard to believe that not so long ago she was the one who couldn't wait to hike into the mountains to go trout fishing on swollen brooks in the spring. The one who pushed him to get his snowshoes on and race her across their frozen fields in the dead of winter. It seemed her diseases had taken her down quickly. On her worst days, Harlan sometimes wished her suffering could end, had even contemplated leaving the whole bottle of pain pills within her reach on the bedside stand. But then there were good days like this one when he wished they could live on together indefinitely.

The teams hit the rink for the last period with a new ferocity; sticks clacking loudly, skates carving deep gashes in the ice. Opponents checked each other into the boards so hard the rafters shook. With two minutes remaining in the game and the score still tied, the officials called *high sticking* on Hinesburg, sending their best offensive player to the penalty box. To win, the Bobwhites had to capitalize on their power play advantage.

As the clock ticked down, the Bobwhites pounded the Hinesburg goalie with a barrage of shots, all of which he masterfully blocked. Martha clapped and cheered between puffs from the oxygen tank. The crowd repeatedly leapt to their feet, arms shooting into the air. Several times she tried to rise on her one leg, but she didn't have the strength. Exhausted, she leaned against Harlan.

With less than a minute left, a Hinesburg player stole the puck and raced toward the Bobwhite's goal. The crowd hushed as he wound up for a shot from just over center ice. Suddenly, Harry's grandson darted out of nowhere, blocked the shot with his body then streaked down the ice on a breakaway. Fans held their breath as he tore past the last Hinesburg defenseman and fired a blistering slap shot over the goalie's outstretched glove into the upper corner of the net.

As the final siren sounded, the Bobwhite crowd exploded. Popcorn, programs, gloves, and winter scarves flew into the air. With great determination, her shoulders trembling, Martha pushed herself up out of her chair. Harlan held her waist, steadying her as they cheered their victorious team.

"Isn't this wonderful?" she said in a weak voice.

"It is indeed." Harlan kissed her on the cheek then helped her slide back down into her blankets.

As the celebration died down and the crowd thinned, the firemen came back and helped Martha and Harlan out of the arena. Mike noticed it was more difficult for Martha to breathe in the cold air. "Do you want to go to the hospital?" he asked.

Martha shook her head and whispered to Harlan, "Take me home. Please."

Harlan looked at the firemen. "She wants to go home. There's nothing more they can do."

"Can we at least give her a ride in our warm ambulance? It'll be more comfortable."

Harlan looked at Martha, who nodded. "That would be fine," he said.

Harlan followed behind the ambulance. Through the arc of windshield wipers clearing wet snow from the glass, he could see Nathan attending to Martha in the back. After all the excitement of the game, it seemed particularly cold and lonely driving home without her next to him.

After the firemen left, Harlan sat with Martha on the edge of her hospital bed. Though it was a struggle for her to breathe, she managed a smile, and motioned for him to come closer. "I want to sleep with you upstairs tonight."

"Really?" he said. "Can we get you up the stairs?"

"Yes. We'll leave the oxygen, all this paraphernalia down here."

For a few moments he stared at the green tubing she had depended upon for so long. "All right. If that's what you want."

"Just you and me," she whispered.

With her thin arm wrapped around his neck, they managed to slowly climb the stairs. Harlan pulled back the undisturbed covers on Martha's side of the bed and helped her slide between the sheets. He climbed in on his side and pulled the comforter up over them.

Martha rolled against him. "Thank you. For everything."

He curled his arm around her. "So good to be in bed together again." He kissed her on the forehead.

Martha smiled then fell into a restless sleep. Harlan felt her weak heart beating against his chest, her breathing rapid and shallow. Somewhere in the middle of the night, she drew her last breath. Soon her heart stopped.

He thought of getting up and making the necessary calls. Instead, he lay there holding her until first light, his eyes closed, imagining them dancing down at the lake on a warm summer night.

For Gina and Luke LeClair

Chapter 5

Myra & Sparky

Her body wrapped in a blue velour housecoat, Myra stood at her linoleum kitchen counter listening to the rhythmic ping of the faucet dripping into the rusted sink. That, the buzz of the TV in the bedroom, and the creaking of the trailer's undercarriage beneath her puffy feet, were the comforting sounds of home. And of course, there was Sparky's high-pitched smoker's wheeze, which she missed when he was gone during the day driving his garbage truck for the sanitation department.

It was just before five a.m., the broken pavement street outside the kitchen window still dark. Myra lowered the fried Spam and cheddar sandwich she'd made into Sparky's tin lunch pail, covered it with a paper towel, and snapped the lid shut. She handed him the pail, cuddled her round belly against his then gave him a kiss on his chapped lips. She felt her Chia Pet-like chin stubble against his freshly shaven cheek.

"Make sure you get home early," she said, staring seductively into his tired eyes. "You know what today is."

Sparky paused for a couple seconds then appeared to force a smile. "Of course, Babe." He tightened the pail under his arm, which was tattooed with an anchor above which read the poorly inked words, *My Girl*. "You going to get all gussied up for me tonight?"

"You bet I am," Myra replied, still making bedroom eyes at him. She re- membered the first time they French kissed in the woods behind the high school. It had made a lasting impression as Sparky was the first guy who had ever been gentle with her.

Sparky pushed open the screen door and Myra followed him out onto the plywood porch loaded with treasures he had salvaged from his route over the years, the centerpiece of which was a faded yellow, bubble-front Skidoo.

Sparky stepped down onto the patchy lawn, turned to Myra, winked, and let out a little hors d'oeuvre of a fart as his final morning salutation. Myra giggled. The door of his pickup crunched as he opened it and climbed in.

A gray squirrel climbed up onto the porch railing and sat looking at Myra. "Don't forget my seeds," she called to Sparky.

"I won't," he said, pulling his door shut.

"Boston's playing the Yankees tonight for the championship. Papi's going to kick their ass!"

"You bet he is," Sparky called as he backed out onto the street.

Myra held her arm out for the squirrel. Its twitchy nose sniffed her familiar fingers then it crept onto her forearm.

"Morning, Mr. Festus," Myra said. She reached behind her and peeled the top off a coffee can of sunflower seeds. She offered Festus a few seeds, which he quickly gathered with his tiny hands then stuffed into his cheeks. He looked up at Myra expectantly.

"That's it, fella. If I give you too many, you'll end up a big heifer like me."

Myra watched Sparky's one taillight disappear down the street, the first pink hues of sunrise appearing through the branches of overhanging trees. She sighed and looked down at Festus, who appeared to be watching the sunrise with her. "When are we ever going to have a baby?" she asked, longingly. She let Festus' tail run through her fingers a few times, then her eyes opened wide. "Maybe tonight's the night."

Myra suddenly began rubbing her belly, startling Festus, who hopped onto the Skidoo. "I swear I can feel my ovaries flarin' again," she said to the squirrel. "And Mrs. Rainville's having a yard sale today. I bet she's got some nice pictures for me."

Feeling edgy, having surreptitiously been off her nerve pills for a few days, Myra pulled a lighter and a bent cigarette stub from the pocket of her housecoat.

Not able to afford her own, she collected butts with a little life left in them from outside the doors of local establishments like the King Pin bowling alley a few blocks away.

Myra steadied her trembling hands around the lighter and cigarette and, after several attempts, lit up. "Yep," she said after a couple of drags. "Going to be a good day getting ready for the big night." She was worried, though, that the timing of stopping her pills might be a bit off. This was hers and Sparky's 25th wedding anniversary and she had convinced herself that tonight her hungry womb would welcome Sparky's tired old sperm like never before. A cute little kid would be born next winter, and she'd finally be able to replace her collection of photos and sports trophies of other peoples' children with some of her own. Not that she didn't cherish her yard sale family, but she knew there was no blood connection.

Myra would have been able to conceive but for that Canadian butcher that messed her up something awful. In her teens she used to get furious about all that, but the pills they'd made her take had mitigated her revulsion at a system that had treated her so poorly. The medicine also muted her ferocious sexual appetite, and somewhere in the haze of cigarettes and squirrels and yard sale pictures, she knew it. So last week she hid her little white pills under her tongue so Sparky couldn't see them when he checked to see if she'd swallowed. Now, on day six of freedom, Myra's dormant lust was rising like a flame through her thick loins. Tonight, hopefully she'd pass through that magical few hours of horny euphoria before the all-consuming anger and torment would again overtake her. Tonight, after Sparky got home from his route, things should be just right.

Myra sat on the duct-taped seat of the Skidoo and watched daybreak brighten over the trailers into a peach-colored glow as if someone was gradually turning up a dimmer switch. She drew in on the last of her cigarette and thought about how far she'd come in her life. Born to an alcoholic mother, Myra had survived with basic assistance from the county. When she was five years old, the county nurse noticed that she was more irritable than the other children. By eleven she was not only hard to control, she had also become disturbingly promiscuous, often aggressively propositioning random men she encountered on the street. And, increasingly, she was obsessed with wanting to have kids. Because she was a charge of the county, Myra was evaluated by Doctor Stampton, who decided she'd never be stable enough to be a competent mother. Besides, with the county trying to catch up with its own needs after the war, he felt the taxpayers didn't need any more illegitimate children to care for. He ordered she be sterilized. The following morning Myra was driven in a cold car two hours north to a nameless clinic in Quebec, where the job was done. "Appendix," they told the confused girl. "Lucky we got it when we did."

After that, Myra's anger and promiscuity became intolerable and she was placed on nerve pills, which went a long way in calming her excesses. It had been a chore to get her to take them, forcing them down her throat in the beginning, later mashing them into applesauce or dissolving them into soups. But by the time she met Sparky, the system had worn her down and she usually agreed to take them on her own. Though it had always been a catch-22. When she was on her medication and balanced, she mourned the loss of the family she never knew and her gregarious, sensual nature was markedly dulled. A couple times a year she'd stop taking the pills, trying to get the old fire back. But as she'd grown older and become obese, Myra found when she was off her meds, the resultant nervous agitation had become harder for her and those around her to take. In a word, she'd exhaust herself. But how sweet were those brief, balanced hours in between.

Myra threw Mr. Festus a few more seeds then walked inside. She lay on the bed and watched *The Price is Right* and reruns of *Gilligan's Island* for most of the morning. After a nap, she went to the kitchen and chiseled enough ice off the Frigidaire's freezer compartment that she could pull the door open. From behind a couple boxes of mixed vegetables, she pulled out a Campbell's soup can which had been converted to a mini safe. She unscrewed the top, pulled out eight one-dollar bills and poured a small amount of change into her hand. She stood calculating for a few moments. She figured Mrs. Rainville might have at least one picture she could afford.

Myra walked into the bedroom, slapped a little cloud of fragrant powder under each arm, threw the bed clothes over the mattress, and pulled on a dress.

She stuffed the rest of her food stamps and half the dollar bills in her pocket, the other half into her bra to save for beer on the way home. She left the trailer and walked down the street being careful not to turn her swollen ankles on the uneven pavement. By the time she reached the main drag, she felt sweaty and tired. She rested against a utility box before lumbering down the sidewalk past the Fill-R-Up toward Mrs. Rainville's. Two men were smoking near the gas pumps, and she eyed the size of one's cigarette butt as he flicked it to the ground.

The sun emerged from behind a cloud as Mrs. Rainville's square, white house came into view. During the summer months, she held a once-a-week tag sale in front and ran a tiny, three-room motel in the back, as close a thing to a brothel the town could ever claim. Myra walked over to several card tables loaded with baby clothes Mrs. Rainville was selling for her unemployed grand-daughter after she'd popped out three little brats in four years, all sired by different boys from the local foundry.

On one table stood several stacks of mismatched dishes, including a cracked souvenir mug from Niagara Falls, along with a tarnished metal replica of the Statue of Liberty with the torch's flame snapped off. Next to it was a wedding photo in a red velvet frame. The bride, in an elegant lace gown, held her dress up to her hip revealing a smooth-as-silk thigh lifted against her man's tuxedo.

"Look at that," Myra pined. She picked up the photograph and held it at arm's length.

"You want to buy it?" Mrs. Rainville snarled from her wheelchair parked in the shadow of her garage. "Five dollar. Real velvet."

Myra frowned and set the photo back on the table. She had only the four dollars to spend and she'd already seen a slinky pink nightgown hanging on a rack next to a set of tires that she just had to get for Sparky. She walked over and held the nightgown up to her bulging torso. She knew it would be too tight, but it was *so* pretty.

Mrs. Rainville drained a Styrofoam cup and dropped it on the ground. Myra walked back and forth between the nightgown and the velvet picture several times. Finally Mrs. Rainville called over to her. "So what d'ya got with you today?"

"Four dollars," Myra said, struggling to model the nightgown in the driveway.

"Any stamps?"

"A few."

"How many?"

"'Bout eight bucks," Myra said, a bit sheepishly.

"'Come on, I know you got more 'n that. It's only the beginning of the month."

"But I got to get beer for tonight. It's our anniversary."

"Ah, don't give me that. It's *always* your anniversary."

"No, tonight's the night. I know it is." Myra tried to balance so she could lift one leg against the nightgown.

Mrs. Rainville shook her head, the lines of her face contracting like that of a dried gourd. Myra waited. She thought about pulling the other four dollars out of her bra but held off.

Mrs. Rainville spat a small wad of brown chew on the ground. "Ah-right, give me the food stamps and the cash and you can take 'em both."

Myra's face brightened. She dug into the deep pocket of her dress. "Oh, thank you." She stuffed the payment into Mrs. Rainville's clawed hand, clutched the nightgown and velvet photo, and hurried down the driveway. She didn't look back for fear Mrs. Rainville would change her mind.

By the time Myra made it back to the King Pin, she was badly overheating. She detoured into the parking lot and rested in the shade against the building's cool cinder block wall. After a few minutes, she began scrounging around by the side door to the bar. So as not to dirty her new nightgown, she draped it around her neck, bent over, and retrieved two decent cigarette butts partially hidden in the gravel.

As Myra righted herself, the metal door suddenly swung open and two drunken fellows from the night shift at the paper mill spilled out into the sunlight.

"Myra, Baby!" one of them called out, lunging towards her.

Myra pushed the salvaged butts into her pocket and stepped back against the wall. "I ain't your baby. I belong to Sparky."

"That old bastard," he said. The men laughed and slapped each other on the back. "You're perfect for each other!"

"That's right," Myra said, as if they meant it as a compliment. Then, with the nightgown flowing behind her, she took off across the parking lot.

Myra's last stop was the Fill-R-Up, where, to her delight, she found several coins in the dirt under the newspaper dispenser. She gathered them up and walked inside where she encountered a display of cheap beer. With the four dollars in her brassiere and her newfound change, she bought a six pack and started home again. On the way, she stopped twice to rest on wooden benches along the street. By the time their trailer was in sight, she was exhausted.

Myra jammed the beer into the fridge, left the nightgown and picture on the kitchen table and took off her sweaty dress. Wearing only her bra, she walked out the back door of the trailer to the small, steel-walled swimming pool Sparky set up for her every summer. Her privacy protected by a tangle of grape vines and honeysuckle bushes, Myra leaned on the handle of a four-wheeler parked beside the pool and flopped into the water. A sizeable wave sloshed over the side onto the parched grass.

"Ahhh..." Myra sighed. She waddled around for a few minutes then settled into the remnant of a chaise lounge Sparky had placed in the pool for her. Her face bathed in golden afternoon sunlight, she fell asleep, rings of water rippling around her in synch with her erratic breathing.

By the time Myra awoke, the sun had fallen behind the trailer next door. Startled she'd slept so long, she pushed herself up hard enough she broke the plastic arm off the chaise climbing out of the pool.

She hurried inside to the kitchen where the Elvis clock over the fridge read almost six o'clock. Sparky would be home any minute and she wasn't nearly ready.

Myra picked up the velvet photo frame and was going to add it to her display shelf over the sink, but then decided not to. Tonight they were going to start their own family. She slipped the frame into the clothesbasket beneath the kitchen table then began scratching the itch under her arm. Her nerve pills had completely worn off. The downward spiral always started with that damn itching. Her pulse quickened. She *had* to get Sparky in bed for their anniversary before things turned ugly.

Myra hurried into their small bedroom, gathered up the dirty socks and underwear strewn about the floor and shoved them under the bed. She'd meant to pick some daisies from her neighbor's garden, but now it was too late.

Peering out the window there was no sign of Sparky so she squeezed a blob of Ever-Curl into her hair and put it up in a half dozen bobby pins. She pulled on the pink nightgown which ripped along a seam in the back, making it look pretty good in the front. Myra pulled her teeth out, dunked them in the pickle jar she soaked them in at night then sprinkled baking soda on them and began to brush.

Just then she heard Sparky's pickup backfire out front. "Oh, no!" She dropped the toothbrush into the sink, squirted a few drops of fixative on her dentures and jammed them into her mouth. They didn't seat quite right, but it would have to do. She peeled a set of long curly eyelashes off a card and stuck them on her lids.

Myra heard the familiar crunch and bang of Sparky's door. She raced through the cluttered kitchen, using her arm to sweep the empty Spam can and crumpled potato chip bag off the table into the trash. She watched from behind the screen door as Sparky lugged two sacks of sunflower seeds up the stairs, dropping them on the porch beside the Skidoo. Mr. Festus watched intently from the limb of a nearby tree.

Though she was starting to feel edgy, Myra threw open the door and wrapped her arms around Sparky. He smelled of old coffee. She knew his last stop of the day was the Trackside Cafe, where all the garbage carried the aphrodisiacal aroma of spent coffee grounds, bacon, eggs, and ketchup, all seasoned with maple syrup.

"You remembered the seed," Myra said, stepping back from Sparky so he could get a full view of her new nightgown.

"Yup." He sat on the Skidoo, and wiped his brow with his hairy arm. "Can you get me a cold beer, Babe?"

Disappointed he didn't notice, but realizing how tired and hot he was, Myra headed for the fridge. She pulled out a can of beer and popped the top. It smelled good. She, too, was going to need a drink to take the edge off her mounting anxiety. She walked back onto the porch, avoiding the soft spot in the plywood, and handed him the beer.

Sparky drained half the can with one gulp. Myra tried to catch his eye with her long eyelashes.

Sparky let out a belch then finished his beer. "Did you get in the pool today? Good day for it."

"Sure did. Almost naked." Myra turned so he could get a better view of her breasts but her itchy armpits distracted her, and worse, distracted him. She tried not to scratch because it irritated Sparky and might make him suspicious. She could feel that old fear and anger building inside. *That goddamn butcher in Quebec.*

"Game's on soon," Sparky said, wheezing when he exhaled. "I hope Schilling has his way with those Yankees tonight."

Myra's heart jumped. She'd forgotten to turn the antenna. She stepped in front of Sparky, blocking his way to the bedroom. "Why don't you take a quick shower? You got time. She nervously pulled the shiny pink fabric up the side of her leg. "Remember what tonight is."

Sparky started to push toward the bedroom where their salvaged TV sat on a couple of stacked wheel rims at the foot of the bed.

"Wouldn't you like to get all clean?" she asked, even though she loved the potpourri of scents coming from his tattooed arms.

Sparky softened. "All right, if it'll make you happy." He turned toward the bathroom. "But I don't want to miss the first pitch."

"Don't worry," Myra said, shoving her hand up under her left armpit and scratching.

As soon as she heard Sparky banging around in their small metal shower, she hurried outside and grabbed the ski pole she used to adjust the TV antenna, as its electric rotor had burned out long ago. Pushing up on her toes as much as she could, she gave the spider-like antenna a shove toward the west, the direction of the Red Sox station. Sparky didn't ask her for a lot, but he wanted the TV ready for him when he got home. Myra hurried back inside. She rushed into the bedroom and sat on the end of the bed to catch her breath. The Fenway organ was blasting out the national anthem as the weak TV picture appeared behind the dusty screen.

"Is it on yet?" Sparky called from the bathroom.

"Just starting," Myra yelled back. In the reflection of the TV glass she saw that one of her eyelashes was crooked, her new nightgown disheveled. She felt frustrated, horny, ugly. Sparky thumped down on his side of the bed, a faded beach towel wrapped loosely around his waist.

Myra tried to get his attention for quite some time, but he seemed interested only in watching the game despite the fact he kept nodding off between innings. By the bottom of the seventh there was no score and Sparky was snoring, his hand clenching a half drunken can of beer that rose and fell on the shelf of his belly.

Myra couldn't take it anymore. She walked into the kitchen, got herself a beer, and stomped out onto the front porch. Pacing back and forth in front of the Skidoo, she eyed a butt on the porch railing but was too agitated to light it.

Mr. Festus climbed onto the railing, cocked his little head, and looked at her empathically. He'd seen her like this lots of times. Myra leaned back against the seat of the Skidoo, and he climbed onto her lap. Patting him calmed her a bit. They sat watching the western horizon, the undersides of white clouds lined with a brilliant orange glow. Soon the street lights came on. She could hear the game on their blind neighbor, Homer's radio across the street.

Myra fidgeted around the front yard, picking stones from between the sparse clumps of grass. Soon, she wore herself out and sat on the top step to rest. Mr. Festus cautiously approached and climbed up on her shoulder.

"*Bottom of the ninth coming up at Fenway,*" she heard the announcer say.

Myra felt a surge of anger and desire. "This is not okay," she said out loud. "I am *not* missing my anniversary." Mr. Festus jumped to the floor as she got up and headed inside. She ran her hands through her hair as she marched into the bedroom and to her surprise, found Sparky sitting back against a pile of pillows watching the game. "Where you been, Babe?" he said. "Bottom of the ninth, Boston's down by one." He reached over the edge of the bed, grabbed a shiny foil chocolate rose he'd hidden from her. "Happy anniversary." He clenched the rose in his teeth.

Myra's eyes lit up, her anger melting into passion. Sparky threw the towel to the floor. Myra lunged on top of him. They began muckling each other as the lead-off batter leaned in. Sparky pulled Myra's new nightgown over her head in an oddly laborious display of lust.

"A slider on the outside corner for strike three and there's one away for Boston."

Sparky kissed Myra while struggling to see the TV.

"Twenty-five years since you took me in the pines," Myra said between kisses. "You was always the one."

"Long fly ball to center field. Johnny Damon's under it and there's two away."

"Those fucking Yankees," Sparky growled. He lifted his head to look at the screen.

"Don't you worry about them," she said, pushing her pelvis against his.

Sparky grabbed a cigar stub off the night stand and lit it. Myra gyrated on top of him.

"Dustin Pedroia swings and lines one into right field for a base hit and the Red Sox have the winning run at the plate."

"Alright," Sparky said. "That's more like it!" He stuck the cigar in his mouth, rolled Myra off of him and climbed on top.

"Oh, Sparky," she said, clutching him.

"Bottom of the ninth. Man on first for the Red Sox and Big Papi, David Ortiz steps to the plate. The crowd is on their feet here at Fenway as Ortiz lines his bat up with center field."

Sparky prepared to do his business, his cigar clenched in his teeth, white ashes falling to Myra's breasts, which sagged to her sides. His pot belly protruded enough it was difficult for him to find his way, but suddenly Myra let out a satisfied moan just as Ortiz swung mightily at Mariano Rivera's legendary cutter.

"Strike one," the announcer called out. *"Big Papi taps his cleats, spits in his gloves and steps back in."*

"You like that, Babe?" Sparky said, wheezing. Beads of sweat covered his brow.

"Go for it," Myra yelled.

"You're right," he said, talking around the cigar. "Tonight's the night!"

"You think so?" Myra cried out, ecstatic that Sparky, too, thought this would be it, on their anniversary in the bottom of the ninth, Ortiz at the plate. Myra cried out in rhythm with the creaking bed springs. Then suddenly her upper plate let go and she started to gag.

"Ortiz swings and blasts the ball high toward right center field."

Myra spit out her dentures. Sweat running down his face, Sparky came, the flimsy steel frame of the trailer rocking to and fro under their weight.

"The center fielder is back, way back on the warning track."

"Yes, Sparky, I can feel it! Tonight's the night."

"Running to first, Ortiz watches the ball come down out of the lights of Fenway. Cabrera leaps in the air and... snags the ball with the end of his glove in front of the Red Sox bullpen."

Before Myra could climax, Sparky rolled off of her and sat, out of breath, on the disheveled bed clothes. He stared at the dejected fans at Fenway.

"Robbed of a home run, David Ortiz looks at the outfield in disbelief. The Red Sox go down three to two. What a tough ending to the ballgame."

After he caught his breath, Sparky pushed himself up against the headboard. Crestfallen, Myra scratched at her armpits, trying to hold her anger at bay. "You want to go again, Sparky?"

Sparky coughed, laughed, and coughed again. Smoke shot from his nostrils and rose to the stained paneling above. "You damn near killed me that time, Babe. Just relax, now." He pulled a sheet up over them and picked up the remote. He clicked to a news station.

In Baghdad, a reporter stood in front of a destroyed schoolyard littered with injured children and soldiers, emergency personnel running to and fro. Across the bottom of the screen a newswire scrolled, announcing the Yankees had just beaten the Red Sox for the American League East Championship.

"Even though the Sox lost, ain't we the lucky ones," Sparky said, flicking his ash to the floor. "Safe and sound in our own home."

Myra sat trembling on the edge of the bed. Inside her brain she heard a young girl screaming bloody murder. She shook her head to get rid of the noise.

The sweat of their love making made her whole body itch. She knew she'd made a terrible mistake stopping her pills. If she could have, she would have scratched her own skin off. "Sweet Jesus," she said, getting off the bed.

"Don't worry," Sparky said, as he clicked back to a recap of the baseball game. "We'll always take care of each other." He watched a replay of Ortiz' almost-home run. "He did his best. Damn Yankees got springs in their feet."

Sparky folded his hands across his belly. "Can you get me a cold one?" he asked, without taking his eyes off the TV.

"'Course," Myra said, part lovingly, part sarcastically. She pulled the other sheet around her waist, walked into the kitchen, and took a cold beer from the fridge. She stared at the cupboard then opened it and pulled her prescription bottle from behind a leaking bag of sugar. She struggled to get the top off then slipped several pills into her mouth and swallowed them.

Chapter 6

Settlement

His arms aching after hours of digging deep in the moist earth, Jed covered the mound of dirt with a carpet of artificial grass then retired to his favorite moss-covered gravestone toward the back of the cemetery. Soon, an older black hearse followed by several luxury cars arrived at the wrought iron gates. Sitting against the headstone, Jed upended a ten penny nail from his overalls' pocket and with its head pushed a pinch of tobacco down into the scorched bowl of his pipe. He lit a wooden match off his belt buckle and drew in the slender yellow flame. As a ring of smoke rose from his mouth, he relaxed against the cold granite, his square-cornered shovel and leather gloves on the ground next to him.

Early May in Vermont was a nice time of year to dig a grave as the earth was soft with winter's lingering moisture. While he worked, Jed enjoyed seeing returning song birds, especially gold finches, redstarts, and bluebirds which built nests in birdhouses he had mounted on fence posts over the years. He also appreciated the delicate scents of apple and lilac blossoms drifting through the cemetery from the abandoned orchard across the hollow.

Jed let out another puff of smoke then grinned. He had sat patiently through many internments, but he'd waited most of his life for this one. If all went well, by the end of the day, some long overdue justice would have been served. It would take a while for the graveside ceremony to conclude, so he pulled his Greek fisherman's cap low over his eyebrows and watched as his friends from the Martin Funeral Home prepared the esteemed Erastus B. Swainbank to be welcomed into the fertile ground.

Jed spent his early boyhood as an orphan under the heavy slate roof of the Hardwick Poor Farm, sleeping in cramped quarters with a couple dozen other homeless folks. Spring and summer, the farm's extended 'family' spent their time planting and tending an expansive garden of potatoes, tomatoes, beans, peas, parsnips, carrots, and corn, as well as several varieties of squash. Daily chores were shared, and when time allowed everyone helped cut and split the twenty cords of firewood needed each year; half for the farm's furnace, half for the sugarhouse for the spring boil. They milked several cows, raised and butchered turkeys, pigs and chickens, and shoveled what seemed like mountains of snow that buried the farmyard from deer season in November till the beginning of trout fishing in April. In addition to long hours of work, the county afforded the children instruction in arithmetic and reading delivered by a strict but compassionate schoolmarm. Over the years, Jed became an avid reader, fascinated with how he could escape into the stories of Charles Dickens, Mark Twain, Robert Louis Stevenson, and James Fennimore Cooper. Never much of a drinker, reading was the one surefire way Jed could distract himself from the hard circumstances of his life.

Though he could never prove it, Jed came to believe his mother's name was Sarah. As he understood it, Sarah's drunken impregnation occurred in a field outside a roadhouse in Sherbrook, Quebec, the work of a handsome Canadian tractor mechanic who, despite hours of drinking swill, still knew a good looking American girl when he saw one. Her former British military father, then an up and coming timberman from Derby Line, would not hear of having a Québécois mongrel in his family. So he imprisoned Sarah at the family's estate on the shores of Lake Memphremagog until she finally delivered after hours of agonizing labor on a moonless summer night in 1946. It was said that a mile down the lake in Newport, Father Renoir heard her terrified screams as he climbed the marble steps to ring the midnight bell high in the tower of St. Mary's Church.

Soon after delivery, the baby, umbilical cord and all, was handed to Sarah's father's most trusted man, who rushed south in a black Packard forty miles to the Hardwick Poor Farm. Wrapped in warm blankets inside a wooden crate, the crying infant was left on the front porch. After a few sharp raps on the door, the deliveryman jumped back into the car and disappeared into the breaking dawn.

After a rough start to his life, Jed was adopted at the age of six by a childless couple from Greensboro who needed help running their struggling grain business. Though he was provided a stable home, Jed longed to look into his real mother's eyes, and figuring out exactly where he came from became an obsession that choked out much of what could have been a more normal life.

Jed watched E.B.'s family standing at the fresh gravesite. He drew in on his pipe, savoring the moment. E. B. was an arrogant lumber baron who made his money the old fashioned way—by working long hours, taking advantage of those less fortunate than him, and refusing to let anyone get in his way. Jed learned what a sharp-edged taskmaster E.B. was after his adoptive family lost their business and he was forced to move back to the poor farm. He hated being back there, living in a stew of angry anxiety most of the time. It came as a relief when he and another boy were sent to work at E.B.'s furniture factory, though he soon experienced firsthand how E.B. extracted a life of hard labor from his workers, most of whom had little idea of the riches he was accumulating.

By the age of twelve, Jed spent what little free time he had trying to figure out whom his birth parents were. No one seemed interested in helping him, and he was thwarted when he tried to research birth records at the county courthouse. Later he took to sneaking into local beer joints and dance halls, gathering any information he could from drunken farm hands and lumbermen. He suspected some of them just made up stories to get rid of him, as there seemed to be a pact to keep him in the dark—a fear, really, on the part of the locals. He eventually came to understand they were protecting E.B.'s family secrets, and no one would risk crossing him.

Reverend Cummings finished a reading of comfort for the departed's family, most of whom had driven up from Pennsylvania and New York, emerging from their Mercedes and BMWs in tailored suits and stylish dresses rarely seen in rural Vermont. Years ago, E.B.'s children had taken as much money as they could and left the Green Mountain State to pursue their lives in distant cities. Regardless of what might have been, Jed was glad he wasn't one of them. It repulsed him to think they might actually be his kin.

When he heard the whole ashes-to-ashes routine, it was time for Jed to stretch his arthritic legs and get back to work. Though he had resisted the cemetery association's offer for many years, he had finally let them buy him a small backhoe to help dig and cover the graves. He kept the machine out of sight when others were around, preferring instead to have only his steel shovel at his side. The backhoe, however, had certainly come in handy.

After the fancy cars had glided down the hill, the undertakers finished up, then stopped by on their way out. Leaning on his shovel, Jed doffed his hat.

Old John Martin rolled down the window of his hearse. "Now, Jed, I'm sure these city folks will want every piece of dirt put back perfectly."

Jed grinned. "Quite the crew, weren't they?"

"Yes, pretty highbrow for these parts. You see the woman whose high heels sunk into that muddy patch?"

Jed nodded. "She wasn't paying very close attention to the Reverend, now was she? She just wanted to get out of here, but don't worry, she'll be able to stand it till the reading of the will tomorrow down to Judge Clyde's."

John frowned. "I never took much of a liking to E.B., hard as he was on the boys working his timber operation. Even so, it galls me these families from down country don't come to visit till some relative with gold in his pockets dies then they make their greedy pilgrimage." He shook his head. "Can't believe they followed E.B.'s wishes and filled the casket with all that booty. They probably thought he'd rise from the dead and jinx the hell out of them if they didn't."

As Jed waited for the undertakers to clear out, the sun edged down through the soft hemlocks bordering the west end of the cemetery, the undersides of cirrus clouds streaked with an orange hue, as if someone had stroked them with a fine brush. A chilly wind blew in from the north causing Jed's knees to begin stiffening.

"'Spose it's out of our hands." Jed pulled on his gloves. "Now you fellas have a good night. I'll get things buttoned up."

"You need a hand with anything?" Mr. Martin asked.

"I'm all set. Just lock the gate when you leave. Don't want any hell raisers in here."

"You bet."

After the Martins drove off, Jed fired up the backhoe and drove it over to the gravesite. Surrounding the perfectly rectangular hole were the foot prints of the grieving family. Jed stared at them, figuring that only his mother, Sarah's, footprints were missing. He'd heard rumors that for years after she gave birth she was cruelly shunned by her family. Eventually, her soul had cracked and E.B. had banished her to a mental institution in the desolate Dartmoor region of southwest England. She'd apparently died there, alone. Jed was only eighteen when he heard of her demise. It ended his quest to find her but left him with rage that threatened to take over his life. He knew he had to find an outlet for his anger, an equalizing force, and he'd been selectively robbing rich men's graves ever since.

Jed turned his gaze to the heavily lacquered, brass-appointed coffin suspended above the grave. He stepped on the rail, triggering the strap mechanism to lower the casket. As it gradually settled into its concrete tomb, he scanned the perimeter of the cemetery. After digging graves for forty years, he knew the outline of every headstone, mound, tree, bush, and fence post. He would notice if anyone was watching from the edge of the woods.

Satisfied, he tossed a duffle bag into the hole, grabbed hold of the bucket for support, and sidled down beside the cement vault. He pulled out his hunting knife and slid it into the casket's seam, breaking the seal. He strained to open the heavy mahogany top. Even though he'd performed this ritual many times, it always gave him the willies when the face of the deceased came into view. E.B. did, however, look fine in his formal infantry uniform, a gleaming silver and gold presentation sword lying next to him.

Jed pulled a canvas tool pouch from the pocket of his barn coat and, with two pairs of jewelry pliers and a freshly sharpened ring cutter, set to work. Two of E.B.'s gold rings slid easily over his bony knuckles, but the other two had to be carefully cut, so as not to waste any gold. Jed placed the rings in a zippered pocket of his overalls then reached into his bag and pulled out a pair of reverse pliers and a hard rubber tongue depressor.

He straightened up and peered over the edge of the grave. It took his eyes a few moments to adjust as he again surveyed the perimeter. Seeing no one, Jed ducked down and went back to work. Taking hold of the corpse's head, he slid the tongue depressor between its teeth, forcing them open. He placed the reverse pliers inside the mouth and ratcheted it open as widely as he could. He looked at the impressive collection of gold fillings, smiling as he touched the two solid gold teeth E.B. was rumored to have had implanted before he left England after The War.

Using dental tools he'd bought at an auction, Jed extracted every bit of gold from E.B.'s mouth and put it safely in his pocket. He rested for a few moments, admiring the colonel's insignia on E.B.'s collar and the ornate meritorious service cross on his chest. After all, he *had* dragged two bleeding comrades from the line of fire in Antwerp, Belgium, during the Battle of the Bulge. With E.B.'s pilfered mouth unceremoniously cranked open, Jed felt a twinge of disrespect. He unlocked the pliers, pulled them out, and forced the gaping jaw closed.

Jed suddenly felt a surge of rage. "I wouldn't be doing this if you hadn't been such a heartless son-of-a-bitch." He drove his finger into E.B's stiff chest. "*You* were the bastard, not me!" He ground his teeth then calmed himself down. "Besides, what good is all this gold goinna' do six feet under?"

Next came a heavy gold commemorative watch and six gleaming coins salvaged from a Spanish galleon forced to the bottom of the Atlantic by a hurricane in the 1700's. Then Jed ceremoniously relieved E.B. of his lavishly appointed sword, which, to his delight, was quite heavy. As dusk descended upon the Pleasant Valley Cemetery, Jed slid the sword into his duffle bag.

Pleased with his haul, Jed took one last look to see if he'd missed anything. The shiny meritorious chest medal was tempting. He lifted the edge of it with his finger. Good and solid. He frowned. "Ah, to hell with it," he said. "That should go down with you."

Jed dusted a little dirt off E.B.'s uniform and thanked him for his overdue generosity. He lowered the lid on the casket, pulled himself up out of the hole, and transferred the stash to his pickup. He used the bucket of the backhoe and a logging chain to lower the cement cover over the vault. He pulled the fake grass off the pile of dirt, and then pushed it back into the grave, back-dragging till the ground was smooth. He would come back the next day and lay out the squares of sod he'd cut and stacked behind the headstone.

He parked the backhoe in its shed, got into his pickup and left.

On the road back to his cabin, his headlights cast eerie shadows which raced past him along the side of the road. Even though he only pillaged the wealthy, he always felt conflicted on the way home; a mixture of anxiety and guilt, conquest and relief. He lit his pipe then rolled down the window, letting fresh air mingle with the sweet cherry smoke. A couple miles down the road, Jed had worked his mind into a good place. "Right thing to do," he said.

Back at his remote logger's cabin, he lit a kerosene lamp and spread the booty out on the kitchen table. He took a block of cheddar cheese and a pork sausage from the fridge, and sat down at the table. He carved off a couple slabs of cheese, sliced the sausage then quickly ate it all. Feeling anxious, he stepped to the window to check the dirt road. Seeing no one, he brought his small balance scale from the pantry and carefully weighed each piece. He recorded the weights in a ledger then slid the items into a deer skin pouch.

Finally, he pulled the sword from the duffle bag. He ran his fingers along the gleaming blade, beautifully etched with a military scene. Years ago, the *Barton Chronicle* had done a story on E.B's distinguished military service, including this ornate British presentation saber given to him by *"the officers and privats of the volunteer infantry as a mark of their esteem."* His pulse quickening, Jed took an antique guidebook down from a shelf and thumbed through it. He located a similar sword and found that, in its near perfect condition, it should be worth eight thousand or more.

Jed looked at his watch. He had to meet Marcel LeBeau at ten o'clock at the abandoned sugarhouse up in Cold Hollow. He popped the cork on a bottle of Canadian whiskey, took a swig and set the bottle on the table. He gathered the booty back into the duffle bag and headed to the door, beside which hung a dark leather holster holding a loaded Colt .45. Though he'd done business with Marcel for years, Jed didn't trust anyone completely. He slid the pistol into his coat and left.

The dirt road leading north to LeBeau's sugarhouse was rough and gullied, causing Jed's pickup to lurch back and forth as he made his way to the end of the road. Marcel's grandfather had built the place such that the border passed directly under the firebox of the evaporator. The old man had gotten a charge out of standing in the States, heaving heavy slabs of Vermont hardwood into a Canadian inferno that produced many a barrel of sweet maple syrup. Of course, back in prohibition days, it wasn't just maple that old Gramps LeBeau made. The still, well hidden in the attached woodshed and vented out through the cupola of the sugarhouse, fooled many a revenuer. And even when a gang of G-men finally shut him down, blasting a hail of shotgun holes through the boiler, the underground delivery tunnel was never found. Despite the government's new high tech surveillance system, the tunnel was just as efficient moving stolen contraband today as it was moonshine back then.

By the light of a kerosene lantern, Marcel looked approvingly at Jed's treasures. "Not bad," he said, touching a pocket magnet to different parts of the sword. They gathered up all the gold and walked over to a small, homemade blast furnace, the "crematorium," as he called it. He melted the gold then poured the gleaming liquid into small lead molds. When he was done, the smelted booty weighed in at a respectable 4.6 ounces.

Squinting, Marcel looked at the sword. "The gold's good, and I can probably unload that to a dealer outside Montreal."

Something banged on the outside of the sugarhouse. Jed stepped back against the wall and slid his hand around the grip of the Colt.

Another bang.

"What's that?" Jed said, feeling the trigger against his finger.

"What's *what*?"

"That banging."

"A loose board or something."

Jed listened carefully. When the noise came again he heard the subtle squeak of a weathered board turning on a rusted nail.

"I'll give you three thousand for the sword and two for the gold. Five grand in all."

Jed frowned. "Antique guide says the sword's worth a lot more."

"May be, if you could find a rich enough buyer." Marcel became impatient. "Look, I'm taking a big risk here. Damn thing's hotter 'n hell."

The board banged again as a gust of wind blew down through the wooden vents in the cupola.

"Seven. For everything," Jed said.

Marcel screwed his face into a knot. He looked the saber over again. "Six. That's it. I ain't talking no more. Gotta' get out of here."

Jed knew when Marcel was done dickering. "All right. Deal."

Marcel disappeared into the attached woodshed and soon reappeared with six thousand in cash. Used American bills, no Canadian. Jed counted the wad of hundreds, fifties and twenties, and stuffed them into his sack. "Okay. Thanks."

He quickly left the sugarhouse, glancing up at the loose board hanging from the peak. Feeling like someone might be trailing him, Jed drove his pickup as fast as he could, bouncing hard on the seat till he swerved out onto the main road. With one hand on the wheel, he took two hundred dollars out of the stash and jammed it in his pocket next to the gun. He made his way along dirt roads past Caspian Lake to Marjorie Stinson's house, eldest daughter of the schoolmarm who had taught him to read. Living alone, hidden away on a back lane in Greensboro Bend, she was the longtime manager of the County Home, the modern descendent of the Hardwick Poor Farm where he had grown up. Though reclusive by nature, she had spent her life helping those left behind during the gentrification of northern Vermont. While so many had lost their farms and could no longer afford a place of their own, the very hills they grew up on had become littered with pretentious ski houses and gaudy hillside mansions. It pleased Jeb to know that Marjorie depended upon him to continue her good works.

Marjorie's house was dark, of course, but she was expecting him. He killed his headlights and drove quietly into the back driveway leading to an old dairy barn. He left the truck idling and found his way to a milk can hidden behind a lilac bush. He pulled the top off, placed the money in a leather mailbag inside and secured the lid. He rolled slowly out of the farmyard, stopping under a large maple tree to watch. Within a few minutes, a familiar shadow appeared from the back stoop and moved across the yard to the milk can.

Satisfied, Jed drove back onto the road, turning his headlights on after he was out of sight of the house. As he sped up, the cool night air felt good streaming through his window. A mile up the road, a coyote stepped out, its beady eyes shining bright in his headlights. A chill prickled along Jed's spine as he slowed the truck to a stop.

For a few seconds, Jed and the coyote stared at each other then it looked away and trotted into the underbrush.

Jed rolled his window up and drove off in silence. Despite all his searching over the years, he had to admit he wasn't *exactly* sure if E.B. was his grandfather. If not, he was close enough.

Chapter 7

Trips to the Woodshed

G rowing up on a hillside farm in northern Vermont, I'd often fall asleep to
the rhythmic ka-thunk of my father splitting firewood in the shed below
my bedroom. I fondly remember one night in second grade when I couldn't get
to sleep. I slid out of bed, tip-toed to the window and pulled the curtain back,
and watched the shadow of my father swinging his axe in the woodshed's light.
I'd never been down in the shed that late at night before, but I had just turned
seven and figured I was old enough.

I snuck down the back staircase to the mud room and pulled on one of my
father's barn jackets, which enveloped me with his familiar scent, a seasoned
mixture of sweat, sawdust, and chainsaw oil. I climbed into a pair of his barn
boots and clomped out the back door into the cold October night.

I hesitated at the shed doorway while Dad finished splitting a stubborn piece
of elm. When I stepped into the light, he leaned his axe against the chopping
block and wiped his brow with his sleeve. "Hi, Bud." He motioned me inside.
"It's late, pretty near midnight. Mother know you're out here?"

"No," I replied, not sure if my adventure was such a good idea.

"Good," he said, breaking into a smile. He sat down on an old kitchen chair
next to a stack of very dry wood. I pulled myself up onto his lap.

"Do you know what you're sitting next to here?"

"Firewood," I replied, confidently.

"Not just *any* firewood. This is our 'family stack.'" He pulled an ancient
looking log from the pile, into which a date had been carved.

I looked at the numbers. "What's that stand for?"

He read the date to me. "August 29, 1864."

My father ran his fingertips along the numbers carved deeply into the wood. "Your great-grandfather cut this log during the Civil War when Abraham Lincoln was President. Oldest piece in the stack. My father told me it came from a grand old sugar maple split in two by a thunderous lightning strike that deafened deer for half a mile. When they cut it up they counted a hundred and fifty-two rings in the trunk."

Dad slid the log over onto my lap. It was dusty and lighter than I expected, but I held it with both hands. I had no idea about the Civil War or who this Lincoln guy was, but it all sounded very important.

"You're holding a piece of wood that sprouted from a seed about 1712, long before the United States was even a country."

"Wow," I said.

Dad showed me other pieces inscribed by family members over the years, including a cracked piece of oak from the day of my grandparents' hasty wedding before grandpa shipped out to England in 1941. There was a piece of white birch from the day President Kennedy died in Dallas into which someone had carved a set of tears beside the initials, JFK. There was also a slab with a likeness of my grandfather's beloved Saint Bernard, accidentally shot by a neighbor during hunting season. Finally, there was a newer piece of wood stripped of its bark into which my name and birth date and that of my older sister were carved.

Growing up, I occasionally caught Dad in the shed on a summer evening just looking over the woodpile, admiring the fruits of his labors. He took such obvious pleasure in how the pieces of beech, ash, maple and birch fit so perfectly together, side by side, completely comfortable with each other. He'd point to a specific piece and tell me exactly which tree it came from, the weather and wind the day he cut it, and how well his chainsaw was running. He'd speak of watching a tall silver maple fall, its leafy branches arcing across the sky like a painter's brush on a blue pallet, crashing to the ground with a whooshing thud. He'd relate the way a stubborn elm twisted hard on its stump, falling—off kilter— from its planned landing, catching in a thatch work of young maples, leaving it at a perilous angle. If a tree became too hung up, Dad would walk around, stare at it from several angles then finally stand back and declare: "We're going to do what George Aiken did for Viet Nam: declare victory and go home." With that he'd load his chainsaw, ropes, sledges and wedges into the bed of his pickup and head for the house.

Dad taught me to cut wood on nature's schedule not my own. If the snows weren't too deep, and the ground was frozen hard winter was a good time to work in the woods. But his favorite was springtime, though if you tried to get into the woods too soon after the frost thawed, the soft, waterlogged ground swallowed your boots like quicksand. There was, however, a short but sweet cutting season just after the ground firmed up, when wild ginger, bloodroot and marsh marigolds budded out and before the black flies rose up in their hungry hordes. During those couple of cool weeks in April we'd trudge into the woods every day and cut up trees blown down by winter's storms. Often, Dad would earmark certain pieces for special occasions, selecting a piece of wood like most people select a fine wine for dinner. An aromatic piece of apple to start the Thanksgiving fire or a perfectly round piece of birch, its bark speckled like a trout flashing in sunlight, to warm the family on Christmas morning.

Once in a while in the woodshed after we'd split and stacked a good load, Dad would offer me a Macintosh from his coat pocket. He'd lean against the family stack and we'd talk, father and son. I don't remember all the details of those conversations but I remember the important lessons he taught.

"This farm is your rock," he'd say with deep satisfaction in his voice. "Everything you need is right here: God and family. You'll find God in the woods; family's in the house."

My senior year in high school I got into an argument with my football coach over how much playing time I was getting and knew the tension between us was becoming disruptive to the team. In the shed one Sunday night before the playoffs, Dad patiently listened to me complain about the coach. After I settled down, he thought about it then nodded his head. "Well," he said, "there's fights in your life it's best you back away from. You'll have to decide if this is one of them." I didn't say another word to the coach and ended up scoring the winning touchdown after he put me in during the fourth quarter.

Another time, when I'd come home from college for Thanksgiving, we were out splitting kindling while Mom and my girlfriend Jenny were stuffing a turkey in the kitchen. Dad knew I was struggling with commitment so I asked him how he'd known Mom was the right woman for him. He leaned on his axe for a few moments then looked at me. "The woman you'll marry will be the one you can't live without." Having been married to Jen for over twenty years now, his advice has served me well. Trips to Dad's woodshed were always a privilege, never a punishment.

Unlike many native Vermonters, Dad never liked to get too far ahead with our wood supply for fear a year might come when we didn't have to cut any. One summer, though, he stepped hard into a gopher hole and snapped a bone in his foot. He limped well into the fall, about as frustrated as I'd ever seen him. It was hard for him to work in the woods or go hunting and it was the only time I ever heard my mother inquire—ever so gently—about whether he had enough wood for the winter. Dad scowled and limped out the back door to the woodshed where he brooded late into the night, splitting a large pile of kindling.

Despite Dad's protestations to the contrary, by late February we all knew the wood supply was going to run out, so one morning at breakfast he announced we were going to go fetch a dead maple that had come down in a gale a few nights before. Knowing there was a lot of snow on the ground, my brothers and I looked at each other questioning Dad's sanity. But before long, we headed up into the hills on our old snowmobiles, toboggans with ropes and chainsaws in tow, and a north wind whipping dervishes of snow all around us. I still remember the look on my mother's face when we arrived home dragging that frozen maple behind us. At the kitchen door, we were greeted by the aroma of hot chocolate and by Mother, who, with hands on aproned hips, shook her head and said simply, "Crazy boys."

Dad dearly loved the countryside where we grew up, and took pleasure in showing us different geologic formations, like unusual boulders found in farmer's fields called *glacial erratics*. He explained they were deposited by the migration of glacial ice thousands of years before. He taught us about the soils beneath our feet and the diverse flower and fern community waving along the forest floor. He demonstrated how certain trees were weakened by acid rain and how mountainsides were scarred and eroded by ATV's.

Each year, we'd gather most of our firewood from our own forest then travel all over northern Vermont to cut our last few "special" pieces. We made many a weekend expedition to different ponds, hillsides and mountain tops, ostensibly to find just the right piece of wood for an upcoming holiday, but it was mostly for Dad to show us the remarkable splendor of our strong but vulnerable Green Mountains.

In the spring Dad would take us trout fishing on Lake Seymour or to the falls in Orleans for the salmon run. He spent as much time scanning the shoreline for an interesting tree as he did watching his bobber and line. One day on Newark Pond he spied a slender "Robert Frost" birch, arced gracefully over the water like a long white fishing pole. We rowed our way over to it and realized it was a good forty feet in length. Undeterred, Dad stood balancing on the seat of our boat cutting off four foot sections which he carefully stacked next to the tackle boxes. "Aren't them beauties?" he said, referring not to the speckled trout we'd caught but to the perfectly round pieces of white birch. "They'll make a dandy Christmas fire." Later that year, we awoke to those same pieces of birch warming the house early on Christmas morning.

One April my Dad got me up earlier than usual and we headed in his pickup to Lake Willoughby. We climbed part way up Mt. Pisgah and watched the sun rise from Pulpit Rock, where we sat high over the lake sharing fresh-cut orange halves. Over the blue-black water an ethereal mist rose silently in the warm morning sun. When we were finished, Dad led us farther up the mountain where we found a good sized limb from a butternut tree that we cut up and took home. As we trudged along he'd teach us how to "read the woods," often stopping to run his fingers along the claw marks of a black bear or the rubbing of a horny buck's antlers on the trunks of young maples.

The year after Mom died, Dad turned ninety-two and the state took his driver's license away because, they said, his eyes had gotten bad. Losing his strength and unable to drive, that fall Dad asked me to take him on one more road trip. He wanted to go up to Irasburg where his boyhood deer camp sat on the east slope of Black Hill. We left his house at five am and drove north through the disappearing November darkness, up over Sheffield heights where a trio of deer watched us pass from the side of the road. "Watch they don't jump 'front of you," Dad said, as I slowed and veered away from them. I guessed his eyes weren't so bad after all.

Just about daybreak we made it to Coventry, crossed the covered bridge spanning the Black River and headed up the old Poutrie Road to where his grandfather's camp was hidden deep in the forest. "There's an ancient black cherry up on the north slope that ought to be outta' gas by now," Dad said expectantly. "I've had my eye on that old beast since I was a kid. Cherry burns like a banshee, gives a wonderful heat. Was one of your mother's favorites, especially around the holidays."

I put my truck in four-wheel-drive, and we climbed up a primitive logging road. "Stay outta' the deep ruts," Dad said, his hands clutched in front of him as if he had the wheel. "Just a little farther and we'll break out into an old apple pasture. The big cherry's on the far end. Beautiful view of Jay Peak up here."

We were both excited, as if we were hot on the trail of a trophy buck. As our pickup dug its way up over the crest of a hill, we suddenly landed on a freshly paved driveway coming up from the other side of the mountain. The pavement led to a fancy iron gate supported by granite posts on either side. Beneath a brass lamp a gold-leafed sign read, "Black Mountain Estates."

I couldn't believe my eyes. Dad's mouth dropped open as he surveyed the strange scene. Beyond the gate was the site of the old pasture, stripped bare of any remnant of how the glacier had left it. A perfectly shaped cul-de-sac curved in front of several Swiss-style homes, each with a two car garage and a lamp-post. My father lifted his hand to his trembling chin and sat in silence. In the distance, Jay Peak, striped with white ski trails, stood against the peach-colored horizon.

Dad's face tightened into a knot. He motioned for us to get out of there. Not wanting to enter the granite gates, I turned around and headed off the pavement back onto the logging road. On the way down the hill, Dad shook his head and stared out the side window. "The only way you can save land is to own it," he said, angrily. "Otherwise the scoundrels'll raze and pave it all. They got no respect."

I think what hurt Dad the most was that an old friend's family had owned that property for over a hundred years and he held them responsible for its demise. On the other hand, Dad was a realist and, though it frustrated him to no end, he knew that a farmer's land was usually his only source of retirement money. He also knew that often it was flatlanders with silver spoons in their mouths who could afford to buy such precious land and keep it open. Even when new owners posted—a practice he detested—Dad grumbled that at least they'd kept it out of the hands of greedy developers.

The ever-present light in Dad's eyes dimmed that day. When we got home, he asked if I'd drag his favorite recliner out of the farmhouse and set it up in the woodshed. He spent his last days surrounded by the things he loved most, gazing out at the unspoiled hillsides of our farm. On his last afternoon, we sat together next to the family stack and watched a parade of Canada Geese v-ing their way south for the winter. There was a hard frost predicted that night, and I tried to get Dad back into the house, but he wouldn't budge. The most he'd let me do was bring him a steaming bowl of corn chowder and a heavy patchwork quilt which I wrapped around him.

Early the next morning I walked down from our place to check on him. I peered inside the shed. There he was, unmoving in his recliner, peaceful as I'd ever seen him. In his lap was a smooth piece of silver maple into which he had inscribed the words "A Lucky Man" and the date he had died. On the floor next to him were the empty soup bowl and his jackknife, which I have carried in my pocket ever since.

Today, with a young family of my own, if I want to get everyone together, all I have to do is light a fire in the woodstove. As soon as the hearthstone is warm they will gather. Our kids usually stretch out on a soft braided rug in front of the stove, and my wife curls up next to me on our couch, which faces the fire.

Not as enthusiastic about heating with wood as I am, my young kids don't exactly run to the woodlot to help out. But I still migrate out to the woodshed after they go to bed to stack 'just a few more pieces.' I usually leave my leather gloves on the work bench, for there is a softness to hardwood I enjoy on my bare hands. Sometimes, in the moonlight, I see my son or daughter watching me from their bedroom windows. They look happy that there will be less of a pile for them to stack come Saturday morning. I trust they'll eventually learn that I am the lucky one for having spent the most time laying logs in for winter. Perhaps late some winter night, when they are old enough to understand, they too will appear in the light of the woodshed and I will show them their very own family stack.

Chapter 8

Reverend Cumming's Storm

B ack when I was still farming, I could tell how bad a storm was going to be by the way our horse pawed the snowpack searching for tufts of grass. He'd been out there for many a Vermont winter, his dark brown coat thickened against frigid Canadian winds that blew down off Mac's mountain, howling as they tore around the corners of our barn. But I never saw him work the frozen ground like he did that particular February afternoon in 1968.

I had just finished chores and was headed to the farmhouse. My warm breath hung in the cold, still air and I could feel the barometric pressure dropping around me. I stopped and scraped frost off the thermometer on the back porch. The red line was just touching eighteen degrees. Perfect for a good Nor'easter.

Back in the house, my wife Elizabeth was in the kitchen laying folded blankets along our damp windowsills to keep out the drafts. I knew she'd soon be brewing a steaming pot of orange spice tea as she always did before the big ones hit. Tea, blankets, and a good book were her armaments against storms.

I walked over to the phone, which sat on a wooden secretary by the kitchen door, and lifted the receiver. It was our night to answer the town fire phone and, in the event of an emergency, mobilize members of the local volunteer fire department. Beatrice, my widowed aunt who lived next door, was jabbering away with her best friend, Nellie Smith, a rather deaf, arthritic maiden who lived in a cabin at the far end of our road. Their voices came over the line so loudly I had to hold the receiver away from my ear.

"Beatrice," I said.

They just kept talking.

"Louder, Dear," Liz said, over her shoulder.

"Beatrice!"

"What is it, Hank? Can't you tell Nellie and I are talking?"

"We're on fire phone duty tonight. Please don't be tying the line up all evening."

"Hank, you boys haven't had a fire call in months. Besides, the telephone's the only pleasure we shut-ins have."

"That's right!" Nellie chimed in. "And we pay New England Tel darn good money for it."

"Well, there're four of us on this party line, and you can make light of it, but we take manning the fire phone seriously."

Nellie and Bea continued talking in their same loud voices.

Liz smiled. "Don't waste your breath."

I shook my head and hung up.

I sat with Liz by the stove and we shared a pot of tea, its warm citrus scent filling the air. We knew Reverend John would soon arrive for his Sunday afternoon visit with my elderly mother-in-law, Eleanor, who lived in the guest bedroom upstairs. John had come to see her every Sunday since her cancer had progressed to the point she could no longer make it to church. Thankfully, she seemed content, finishing up a good life surrounded by piles of her beloved books, on top of which stood framed photographs of friends and family and a vase full of yellow plastic daffodils.

Two years older than I, John Cummings grew up on a neighboring farm. He was like a big brother to me and was especially kind when my dad died of a lung hemorrhage from consumption when I was nine. After that, John became my constant companion. He taught me how to fly fish for trout on deep stretches of the Missisquoi River and showed me the secret of his legendary side-arm baseball pitch behind our barn where the Slacken boys couldn't watch us. And the summer I turned thirteen, in the privacy of his father's chicken coop, he taught me how to kiss a girl with the assistance of his older and quite amorous sister, Kate.

John idolized Kate and spent as much time with her as possible. They often rode their horses together; hers a temperamental white stallion, his a dark, sure-footed Morgan. They always seemed so happy together until the summer of her senior year in high school when everything changed. They took a camping trip on horseback up into Quebec, and afterward John and Kate seemed to inexplicably grow apart. She soon took up with that wild Billy Marshall boy and stopped hanging out with John all together.

John became increasingly worried about Kate as she drank and caroused at weekend dance halls with Billy. Then, on a hot, sticky July night near their farm, drunk and crazy, Billy mowed down a row of guard rails before hitting a cement bridge abutment with his pickup, catapulting Kate through the windshield. The truck rolled over her on the way down the embankment before it landed in the waters of Sheldon Creek.

Half out of his mind, Billy took off and left Kate dying on the stream bank. Up the road, John heard the crash through his open bedroom window and ran barefoot to the scene. He followed fresh tire ruts down the bank to where he found Kate, her body twisted in a thatch of alders. Aghast at the sight of her, John realized her neck was broken and she was bleeding from her ears. Barely able to breath, he vainly cried out for help, his voice lost in the rush of the stream. He struggled to free her, but it was hopeless. Swarmed by ravenous mosquitoes and stained with her blood, John fell back into the mud and gently pulled Kate's limp body onto his. He supported her head, carefully clearing tangled hair and glass from her face. He later told me that after she stopped breathing he felt her spirit surround them, a peaceful, calming presence that lingered for some time.

As Liz and I finished our tea, we heard John's familiar knock at the front door. Greeting him, we realized it had started to snow. He brushed off his coat, walked in and took off his green wool cap.

"Dandy sermon this morning, Reverend," I said.

"Thank you, Hank. According to you, I've never preached a bad one. I wish it were so."

"Well today's was one of your best. As you said, we all need to practice more forgiveness before we meet our maker."

"I believe so." He glanced up the staircase. "How's Eleanor?"

Liz spoke softly. "She was up much of the night again with that awful pain in her back. Doc says the tumor's gone into her bones."

"We try, but she's stubborn about taking the pain pills," I said. "She'd rather read the Good Book than take codeine."

John nodded. "Good for her. The old gal knows what she's about." He took hold of the handrail and climbed the squeaky stairs.

While John visited with Eleanor, Liz began fixing her famous chicken biscuits for dinner. I sat watching the firebox of the woodstove and thought about John. In the months after Kate died, he seemed numb, mostly kept to himself. We didn't fish or play baseball the rest of that summer. And I remember being amazed that he went to see Billy after he got out of the hospital. He'd supposedly sobered up after losing an arm and an eye from the wreck. John told me he was tortured by what Billy had done but in order to save himself he had to find a way to forgive.

Finally on a warm September afternoon, John came by the farm and asked me to go partridge hunting. He seemed nervous as we walked a mile or so up to an abandoned apple orchard. As we approached, a grouse thundered up from the underbrush right in front of John. A crack shot, he never raised his gun. Instead, he turned to me, his face full of angst and sadness. He said I had always been his best friend and that if he didn't tell me about what happened between Kate and him on their camping trip in Quebec he would surely die. It was the consummation of his deepest, most forbidden desire that, in the end, had broken them apart. He looked me in the eye, swore me to secrecy, and told me the rest of the story.

As John finished, his anguish was overtaken by shame. Struggling to catch his breath, he covered his face with his hands and wept. I was disturbed by what he told me but tried not to show it. I reached out to put my hand on his shoulder but he began pacing. He said he was consumed with guilt, didn't know what to do with himself, and the only relief he got was talking to Eleanor Howard, his Sunday school teacher. After several discussions with her, he said that he had found his calling. That the only possible path to redemption was to become a man of the cloth.

I tried my best to comfort him, to help relieve a depth of pain I had never witnessed before. Unfortunately for both of us, he would never allow us to speak of it again. Instead of drawing us closer, the knowing silence worked to separate us.

Liz turned from the kitchen counter. "You'd better put the coffee on. John will be down soon."

I left the warmth of the woodstove, readied the percolator then leaned on the edge of the sink. Outside the window, I watched snow rapidly accumulating on our bird feeders. As I enjoyed the aroma of fresh coffee, my thoughts returned to John.

After high school, I stayed on the farm and he went off to college, eventually graduating from divinity school. John spent several years working at a mission in the bowery of New York then came back home to become pastor of our Community Church. John lived alone in a small house he built on a hill overlooking the cemetery where Kate was buried. He devoted most of the week to visiting homebound parishioners, counseling young people, and serving as a volunteer firefighter. But then nobody would see him for a couple of days. I knew that he'd go up to his hunting camp in Berkshire where he worked in the sugar woods, rested, and I presumed talked with God in the quiet of the forest as he prepared his Sunday sermons. I suspected there were other reasons behind his regular escapes, but out of respect, I kept to myself. After all, Reverend John was somehow connected to the Divine; a saver of souls—his and ours.

Out deer hunting one fall, the Slacken brothers passed by John's cabin and said they heard him clambering around inside, arguing with someone they figured wasn't actually there. "Stinking drunk," they said he was. We ignored them, laid it to their still being jealous over John's pitching prowess in high school. And to be honest, we didn't want to know anything bad about John that would injure our myth. We needed him up on that pedestal for our own good, though certainly not for his. As for me, I struggled with our bond of secrecy, wanting so badly to find a way for him to get help. But all I could seem to do was take it to God in my prayers as I lay awake many a night.

By the time John came downstairs, the coffee was ready and Liz had a chocolate brownie waiting for him. As usual, he sat by the woodstove in my father's Morris chair. He put a couple pieces of dry birch on the fire then stared into the stove, his large blue eyes watching the white paper bark curl into the flames.

We chatted a bit then John finished the brownie, and downed the last swallow of coffee. He walked to the front door, put his green cap back on, and said goodbye.

"Thank you," Liz said, holding her sweater tightly about her. "Your visits mean so much to Mother."

John paused at the storm door, its glass covered with frost. "I'm glad, Liz. Truth is I thought I'd die after I lost Kate. As you know, your mother has given me great comfort. She has been my greatest spiritual guide."

John pushed the door open and stepped outside. From the darkened sky, millions of snowflakes fell through the dark branches of our farmyard maples.

"You get right home," Liz said.

"I've one more stop at Nellie's up the road. Won't take long; she's usually on the phone." He grinned at Liz. "And she can't make brownies worth a darn."

John walked toward his Jeep. "Going to be a whale of a storm," he called back. "I can feel it."

Liz watched John drive off then closed the door. "Do you think he'll still come to visit after Ma passes?"

"I expect so. I think we'll always be close to John."

"I hope so, though I worry about him sometimes."

"I know. So do I."

By four o'clock I was ready for chores. I slipped a couple of brownies into the pocket of my barn coat and headed outside. The storm was intensifying, large snowflakes appearing against the side of our red barn as though someone had splattered white paint off the bristles of a brush.

As always, my ladies were waiting for me. I let them into the barn where a litter of kittens milled about anticipating a meal of fresh spilled milk. I cleaned the first set of teats with a soft cloth soaked in warm water and iodine then applied the slender suction tubes. While the machines milked, I raked manure from under the cows onto the worn blades of the gutter cleaner.

Around six, chores half over, I sat on an overturned pail, leaned back against a wooden post and rested. A calico kitten appeared beneath me and clawed its way up a pant leg into my lap. As I petted her silky fur I looked around the barn my forbearers had built nearly a hundred years before. It was a good solid structure, though I heard the upper post and beams creaking in the strong wind.

I saw the floodlight come on in the yard and assumed Liz was on her way with hot coffee. I nudged the kitten off my lap and straightened up just as the door burst open. Liz rushed inside amidst a gust of swirling snow, her boots untied, her coat unbuttoned. "Hank!" she called out, pushing the door closed behind her.

"What is it?"

"Fire phone. Accident over by Tucker's Bridge."

"Bad place, especially in this weather." I glanced at the milking machines. "I'll finish up here. You go."

"Thanks. Did they say what kind of wreck?"

"All I know is the milk truck hit somebody. Frank's gone to get the fire truck. Marilyn said Joe's down in town so he'll bring the ambulance. They want you to go straight to the scene."

I was one of the few firemen who'd ever taken a first aid course, so I was usually sent to do the medical work on accident calls. "I'll be back soon as I can."

"Be careful," Liz said as she walked toward the cows.

When I lifted the latch on the door, the wind blew it open so hard it swung around and slammed against the wall, rattling the glass. Outside, snow blew at me with such force I had a difficult time crossing the farmyard to my pickup. I quickly brushed off the windows and headlights, climbed in and fired her up. The cold hydraulics squealed as I raised the plow. Even though the engine was cold, I turned the defrost on full blast and, leaning forward over the dash, could just barely see. With my window open a crack, I started out of the yard toward Tucker's Bridge, several miles away.

Joe Tetrault, our fire chief, came over the radio, said he was heading to Lester's Garage to pick up the ambulance. He advised the roads were real bad and to take it easy. I reached behind the seat and felt for my canvas first aid pack, buried beneath old tractor catalogs, crushed coffee cups, and a collection of tools. I pulled the pack out and set it on the seat next to me.

Already a foot on the ground, heavy snow swirled in my headlight beams. It was difficult to see the edges of the road as the town plow hadn't made it out as far as our place. I dropped my blade and plowed my way across town. As I approached the scene, I made out a set of tire tracks that zigzagged through the snow then disappeared off the road. A brilliant red flare was stuck in the top of a wooden guardrail post. Standing next to a pickup with a red light on its roof was Jim Mayville, another fireman. I pulled over and rolled down my window, snowflakes blowing across my dash. Jimmy's long curled mustache was encrusted with snow.

"Fred Lucier's milk truck's off the road, and there's a damn drunk down there in the trees. Rig's smashed. You guys'll have to cut him out." Jimmy wiped his mustache with the back of his hand. "Fred said the car swerved right into him. He tried to miss him, but the guy plowed into his rear axle and went over the bank."

"Fred okay?"

"Yup. Just a little shook up."

"The other guy?"

"Front end's demolished. He's trapped."

"Anybody we know?"

He shook his head. "Don't think so. It's a mess, not even sure what kind of vehicle it is."

I grabbed my flashlight and first aid pack, and got out. The heavy smell of diesel fuel swirled around me.

"I don't know if you can do much for him, but I'll take you down."

I followed Jimmy past the milk truck, which lay on its side in the ditch. As we stepped off the road I saw Sheriff Henry's cruiser pull up on the bridge just beyond us, followed by the ambulance and our old pumper, its revolving red light sparkling through the falling snow.

Jimmy and I held onto a broken guardrail cable as he led me down an embankment to a thick stand of trees at the river bank. As we approached the wreck my foot broke through a soft spot in the frozen ground flooding my boot with ice water. We continued through twisted saplings to the vehicle, which was nosed into a cottonwood tree.

Jimmy climbed around to the driver's side, the door and a portion of the roof having been torn off. He lifted a branch out of my way. Wet snow fell onto the hot engine making an eerie hissing sound. The smell of whiskey emanated from the vehicle.

The man was pinned at an odd angle between the bent steering wheel and the dashboard. I set my first aid pack on the crumpled hood and pulled out my stethoscope. I slid the scope inside the man's coat and listened to his chest. I felt the ends of his broken collar bone grinding together. He moaned in pain, his lungs rattling with each breath. His heart sounded distant and weak. I felt for a pulse at his wrist. Thready at best.

"Goinna' make it?" Jimmy asked, not looking at the man.

I shook my head. "Doubt it. Got a head injury, breathing's bad and both legs have compound fractures. He's bled all over the place."

I felt badly but realized I couldn't do much except try and comfort him.

"He's probably too drunk to feel much," Jim said.

The man moaned again, raising his hand as though trying to his wipe his eye.

"I think he can feel plenty," I said.

Chief Tetrault, Sheriff Henry, and a couple other men made their way down the snowy embankment to the wreck.

The sheriff shook his head. "Smells like a damn still." He looked at me and lowered his voice. "He gone yet?"

"Almost." I kept my hand on the man's arm.

"Any idea who he is?"

"No. Too banged up. Half of him is crushed under the dash."

The sheriff looked at the victim. "Hate to leave him here. I'll call for Wheeler's wrecker, though I don't know if he can pull him out of there with it storming like this." He glanced up at the sky. "Though if this keeps up it'll be even worse getting him out in the morning."

"Hank, soon as he's gone, you give us the go ahead and we'll have Wheeler try and drag the wreck back up onto the road." The sheriff glanced at Chief Tetrault and the other firemen. "Come on, I don't want you gettin' hurt down here." They all climbed back up the bank.

I maneuvered myself so I could check the man's pupils to see how much life was left in him.

With my flashlight in one hand, I gently brushed glass from his eyelid.

As my thumb lifted his lid, a large, dilated blue eye stared straight at me. For a moment it so unnerved me I shuddered and looked away, my gaze catching a green wool cap jammed in the corner of the dashboard. I'll never forget the horrible feeling that shot through me like a gun blast to my chest.

I slowly looked back at the man's face. "Oh, God—"

"What is it?" Jimmy asked.

"It's John."

"John who?"

"John Cummings."

"Can't be—" Jimmy said, cautiously stepping closer.

As I leaned against the windshield frame, John's other eye opened. His lips, stuck together with dried blood, cracked apart and started to move.

Shocked and not sure what to do, Jimmy struggled back up onto the road, yelling to the other men. Through the howling of the storm, I heard the pain, the utter disbelief in their voices as they got the news and raced back down the bank.

John's lips moved but made no sound. I leaned forward and listened. His breath was a strong mixture of whiskey and blood.

"Please, forgive me," he said in a barely perceptible whisper.

"John, we're right here with you. The guys are going to get you out." I took his hand. His flesh was cold. My heart pounded furiously. "It's going to be okay."

Jimmy looked at me, a sort of vacant terror on his face. "What can I do, Hank?"

"Have the boys bring down the extrication tools. Got to pull this dashboard off of him. And get some blankets."

Firemen quickly retrieved the equipment. Sheriff Henry and the others surrounded the Jeep. Jimmy took off his fire coat and held it over John and me as they worked to free him. One man climbed up into the cottonwood and tied off a heavy come-along which they used to pull the steering wheel off John's chest.

As the men strained and metal creaked, John's eyes closed. His head slumped against my shoulder. He was still alive, but barely.

"Jimmy, you're Catholic, right?"

He nodded.

"You got a cross or one of those rosaries with you?"

He unzipped his coat and pulled a silver cross hanging on rawhide from under his shirt. "What do you want me to do?"

I looked at John's mottled face then back at Jimmy. "He asked me to forgive him, so I'm going to."

Jimmy pulled the necklace over his head and handed it to me. I glanced at the men who were all staring at John. "Bow your heads," I said.

Ice fell from Chief Tetrault's fire helmet as he took it off and tucked it under his arm. Sheriff Henry, a friend of John's and mine since first grade, removed his wet Stetson. I reached out and held the cross on the top of John's head then cleared my throat as best I could. "Here, in the plain sight of God, John Cummings, one of the best men we've ever known, you are forgiven for *all* your sins, forever and ever." My voice broke.

Each man reached forward and laid a hand over mine. I looked at the crown of hands on my dear friend's head. "I'm *so* sorry I wasn't there for you when you needed me most. I love you, John. Always have."

For a few moments there was a pause in the howling of the storm, a frozen stillness there by the stream. As the men stepped back one by one, I unzipped my coat, leaned forward and wrapped my arms around my friend. I held my warm chest to his. I envisioned John drinking in his Jeep alone after visiting Nellie. He had seemed so normal coming to see Eleanor, talking with us in the kitchen. I could hardly believe what I was witnessing.

I tried to keep John warm until he'd taken his last breath. As the men shivered with cold and grief, I think in our own ways, we all felt his spirit move among us as it rose into the stormy night. We covered John's body with several blankets then Sheriff Henry spoke to us. "We failed our friend when he was alive. The least we can do now is bury Reverend John with the honor and dignity he deserves."

The sheriff took the whiskey bottles out of the Jeep then slogged across the icy creek and dumped them in some thick bushes on the far side. When he came back to us, he looked across each of our faces. "This will never be spoken of again. *Ever.*"

It seemed like the whole county came to town for the funeral. It was a warm winter day and the bright sun imbued the high snowbanks with a magical blue hue. Every school in the district was closed that afternoon and the farmers' cooperative shut down on a weekday for the first time anyone could remember. Led by Sheriff Henry's cruiser, John's funeral procession moved slowly through town to his church, his flag-draped casket riding high in the hose bed of our old pumper.

The Bishop came from Burlington to preside over a service filled with music, flowers and profound sadness. Aunt Beatrice came to the funeral with Nellie, the last person to see John before the accident. For the first time in nearly a year, with great determination, Eleanor struggled downstairs and rode to church, sitting between Liz and me in our pickup. At the altar, she abandoned her walker, knelt at John's casket, and laid a bouquet of plastic daffodils by his head.

Many people lovingly eulogized John, speaking of the comfort he gave to so many. There was a profound communal grief at his loss and I'd never seen as many men and women cry as I did that day. My own grief was sickening, knowing I had been unable to relieve John of his unspeakable guilt.

More than twenty years later, we've retired from farming and arthritis has taken over most of our joints. Our horse is long gone and our dairy barn stands dark and silent. Still, when a bad Nor'easter is coming our way and folks refer to Reverend Cumming's Storm, most people think it a testimony to the power of Mother Nature and to a great man who sacrificed his life out ministering to the weakest of his flock.

For those of us whose lives forever changed that night, it means far more.

Chapter 9

Executive Session

H arry Thurber stepped closer to Claude. "We best be going in before they come out and get you."

Claude rolled his empty pipe in the palm of his hand but said nothing.

"I know you're about at wit's end, but you've got to get this over with."

Claude slipped his pipe into the shirt pocket of his overalls. "I don't know, Harry, I'm so worn out my teeth are tired."

"Come on, now. We've fried bigger fish 'n this."

Claude followed Harry into the town hall meeting room. Claude sat in the first chair by the door. Harry sat at the table and leaned his cane against the wall. The heavy steam radiator beneath the window hissed and cracked, taking the chill off the late October afternoon.

Frank Pelini, the recently elected selectboard chairman, took off his bifocals and set them on the worn oak table in front of him. It had been a difficult, politically charged investigation, and he didn't relish delivering the news. He looked at no one in particular when he spoke. "I have given this matter a great deal of thought. After careful consideration of the facts, my recommendation is that Claude Demers be relieved of his duties as road commissioner and never drive a piece of town equipment again."

The deep lines of Claude's forehead sagged. He sat motionless, leaning on one arm of his chair, the bowl of his pipe tugging at his pocket.

Reg Simons shot out of his chair. "What the hell you talking about? Claude's been taking care of our roads for half a century. He's the best snowplower in

Vermont, for Christ's sake." Reg leaned across the table closer to Pelini, who had moved to town from New Jersey two years before. "You ain't taking his plow away from him."

"Settle down, Reg," Pelini said.

"I ain't going to settle down. You outsiders come in here, think you know how to run everything. Well you've got another thing 'a comin.'" Reg thumped back into his chair.

Pelini picked up his glasses and motioned around the table. "You all grew up here, have known each other your whole lives, but that doesn't obviate the fact that last summer Claude's carelessness nearly took the life of a young girl. It's already cost the town fifty thousand, and it could be years before the matter is finally settled."

Reg shook his head. "He's never been charged with a crime. Even Judge Thompson said Claude, the kid, and her parents were all partly to blame."

"Be that as it may, Claude was driving the town grader when the blade cut into Missy Rosenthal's abdomen causing her to bleed nearly to death in front of her parents."

Claude fiddled with the arm of his chair. "I never meant to hurt that little girl. Street was closed off. I put them barricades up myself. She come out of nowhere from behind a pile of gravel. I tried to stop..."

Claude choked up. The whole ordeal had nearly killed him. Forty-eight years with nothing more than a few bent mailboxes, and then this.

"'Course you couldn't stop," Reg said. "That kid ran right out in front of you." He turned and glared at Pelini. "Besides, if that'd been some local farm girl instead of a rich tourist's kid we wouldn't be sitting here."

Pelini ignored him and continued. "What if this winter Claude runs over someone with his plow? We could never defend the town. How could we live with ourselves?" He looked at Claude. "I've discussed this at length with the town attorney, and he thinks—"

Reg slammed his fist on the table. "That lawyer's nothin' but one of your flatlander friends. Why should we care what he thinks?"

"The town's fortunate to have Tony working with us. You didn't have a real attorney before I brought him in."

"We were a hell of a lot better off, too," Reg said.

"Look, people," Pelini said, "some things *have* to change around here. You can't hang on to all your old, provincial ways."

"Like what?" Harry asked, indignantly.

"Like granting building permits and paving driveways for nothing for your friends, while ignoring the needs of new people who've decided to move here." Pelini's face tightened. He looked at Reg. "Like opening your hardware store any old time, night or day for your cronies, but not staying open an extra five minutes on Christmas Eve so I could get batteries for my grandson."

Reg looked away.

Pelini composed himself. "You have to consider how your actions appear to people from the outside world."

"I don't give a goddamn what they think of us," Reg said.

"Well you'd better start because they're all around you. Those tourists who drive up here from the cities spend millions of dollars on maple syrup, hunting licenses, skiing, all sorts of things. They won't keep coming if their children are in danger of getting run over by a road commissioner with bad eyes."

"I got new glasses since the accident," Claude said, touching his thick black frames.

Harry cleared his throat. The room became quiet. "If I follow your logic, Mr. Pelini, because I'm nearly eighty years old, got a gimp leg, and am pretty set in my ways, soon you'll be replacing me as fire chief."

"That's not the issue we're here to discuss."

Claude sat up in his chair, pointed his finger at Pelini. "Now you listen here, there ain't a fire chief in this state more respected than Harry Thurber. And don't be making fun of Harry's bum leg. He got that in France fighting for our country. Got nothing to do with his age."

"Besides," Reg interjected, "which arm of the military did you serve in?"

Pelini ignored them both. "I'm not advocating replacing the old town crew all at once, but I am saying you've got to realize these inevitabilities. People are worried about the town being ruined by another law suit. In large part, that's why I was elected chairman of this board."

There was a knock on the door.

"Come in," Pelini said.

Dressed in a dark pinstripe suit and polished black shoes, town attorney Tony Malto stepped into the room, set his briefcase on the table and sat down.

"Great—" Reg said under his breath.

Mr. Malto opened his briefcase and took out a yellow legal pad.

Pelini looked at him. "Things aren't going particularly well."

"These are difficult matters." Mr. Malto unbuttoned his suit jacket. He looked around the room. "Would it be helpful if I spoke to the matter at hand from the town's legal point of view?"

"Aren't *we* the town?" Reg asked.

"Yes, a representation of it, but North Branch has grown dramatically. It's not the same sleepy town it was twenty years ago. It has been *discovered,* if you will, become a favorite getaway for down country people. In fact, many of them are winterizing their vacation homes and moving here year round."

"Yeah," Reg said, "they're building fancy houses, ruining hay fields our families have farmed for generations."

"I agree some over-development has been done by out-of-staters. On the other hand, they have preserved a lot of land because they can afford to build a house on a hundred acres and keep the rest of the property open. Some of the densest, and in my opinion, worst development has been done by local developers who jam far too many trailers onto a field, completely changing the landscape. They couldn't do it if local farm families weren't throwing in the towel and selling out."

"If they paid our farmers a decent price for milk their kids would stay home and keep farming, not run off to the city." Reg said. "Besides, locals got a right to live however they want."

"I understand how you feel, but as a public municipality we can't condone double standards."

"T'ain't a double standard. Native's got more rights than outsiders."

Mr. Malto opened a file folder. "I'm afraid that's not true."

Harry leaned forward. "Thanks for the civics lesson, but what's all this got to do with Claude?"

Mr. Malto turned to Harry. "Many locals believe what happened to Mr. Demers could have happened to anyone, that they were all victims of bad circumstance. Other people, particularly summer folks, feel much has been overlooked, that a danger is being swept under the rug." He looked at Claude. "Is it not true, Mr. Demers, that well before the accident you were found to have poor vision with the glasses you were wearing that day?"

Claude reluctantly nodded in the affirmative.

"And didn't the doctor find that you had been having dizzy spells off and on for some time, including while working?"

"He found all kinds of things wrong with me, but now he's got my blood pressure and sugar under control."

"The point is you continued to work while physically disabled, and that calls into question your judgment. Eyesight is pretty essential for a truck driver."

"I didn't realize anything was wrong with me. I never stop for very long. I get up early, do my work, and get home at night to tend to Mary. Her paralysis is getting real bad. Deer season and maple sugaring are the only times of year I take off. That's when her sister comes down from Quebec to watch her."

Harry looked across the table at his oldest friend. "I'll bet you've never taken a Thanksgiving, Christmas, or New Year's off, have you Claude?"

Claude shook his head. "Can't. Weather's always bad and with all them people on the roads, I got to keep 'em clear." He looked at the floor. "I would have gone to Doc sooner if I'd known I could hurt someone."

Mr. Malto leaned toward Claude. "Mr. Demers, we are in no way negating the good things you have done, the service you've provided to the town. But we—Mr. Pelini and I—are deeply concerned with preventing another accident. As difficult as it is to say, we just don't feel you're safe."

As the spirit drained out of him, Claude hung his head.

Pelini spoke in a subdued voice. "Would you like to say anything else to the Board before we go into executive session?"

Claude slowly came to his feet. "All I ever wanted to be was a road man." He turned to Harry. "We been through some awful storms together, haven't we? Like the blizzard of '68, forty-two inches in twenty-four hours. Snow came down so fast you couldn't believe it. And I had my trucks freeze up just once, in '71 when the mercury hit forty below five days in a row. The night the plows froze, the globes on the street lamps burst when the bulbs came on at dusk. Had shattered glass on the sidewalks in the morning."

Chairman Pelini waited a few moments. "Is there anything else?"

Claude took a step forward. "I need to work another year till I'm sixty-five to get my full pension. That would help out taking care of Mary. The visiting nurses are wonderful, but they aren't cheap. I just can't do it all myself." He paused, looked Pelini in the eye. "Would you see if you can keep me on 'till my birthday next summer?"

Attorney Malto looked away.

Pelini looked over his glasses. "Thank you, Claude. You may go home while the Board deliberates. We'll call you as soon as a decision is made."

Harry stood. With his cane in one hand and his other arm guiding Claude, they walked out of the room.

In the hallway, Harry paused. "Whatever happens in there, you're one of the best men I've ever known. I'll do what I can."

Claude nodded, pulled on his overcoat, and walked outside where a cold wind lifted piles of leaves, swirling them around the parking lot like small tornados.

It was late afternoon when Claude got home. It was Mary's bath day and Angela, her visiting nurse, was still with her so Claude walked to his workshop attached to the side of the barn. He paused at a pile of unsplit firewood then stepped inside.

At his workbench Claude filled his pipe with tobacco and looked out the small, cob-webbed window at the rocky pasture cleared over a century ago by his great grandfather. As he drew the flame of a match into the bowl, a few light snow flurries began dancing in the air. He leaned against the bench and perused the rack of old tools and the wood-handled saws hanging from the hemlock rafters.

Claude took his Winchester down from the deer antler gun rack mounted over the bench. He wiped the barrel with a chamois cloth moistened with gun blue then walked outside. He tightened the collar around his neck and, with his pipe clenched in his teeth, headed across the pasture to the stump of an old sugar maple he'd cut last summer, just after the grader accident. He sat down and laid the rifle across his lap. He felt the cold steel of the barrel through his pants.

Claude looked back at the house and thought about how much he wished he could make Mary well again, for both of them. He was grateful that over the years they'd pretty much accepted their disappointments without blaming each other. That night long ago at the county fair he'd found himself a damn good woman.

As an early snow fell gently on the field, a slender red fox ventured out of its hole and pounced on some poor creature next to an abandoned hay bale. A hawk soared over the tall pine trees at the top of the knoll and a trio of chipmunks chased each other in and out of the stone wall at the edge of the woods.

Sitting on the cold stump relieved the burning at the base of Claude's spine, the nagging pain and numbness down the back of his right leg. Probably way too many years riding rough roads in stiff dump trucks, and pushing and pulling countless stuck rigs out of thick spring mud. Claude rapped his pipe on the side of the stump, slid it into his pocket and closed his eyes.

The hillside had turned dark and cold by the time Claude was aroused by Angela's voice. As he straightened his stiff back, he realized he'd fallen asleep, his hands still clenched around the gun, his overalls covered with a thin layer of snow.

Angela stood beside him, holding her coat tight about her. "Shirley called from the town hall. They want you to come back down."

Claude dusted the snow off his rifle. "Thanks," he said, standing. "I must have dozed off."

They walked back across the pasture toward the house. Angela had been a great caregiver for Mary and a kind buffer for him. As Mary's multiple sclerosis had worsened, her daily routine had become more and more uncomfortable for him. Angela had helped both him and Mary maintain as much of their dignity as possible.

"A lot of people are rooting for you," she said, as they reached the front porch. "Good luck, now." She climbed into her Subaru and drove off.

Claude walked inside and leaned his rifle against the coat rack. He was glad he hadn't needed it.

Mary was lying on the sofa in the parlor, her favorite blue quilt tucked under her chin. "Gettin' cold out," Claude said, walking over to her. He gently touched her cheek.

Mary opened her eyes.

"I'll stoke the fire then I've got to go back down, see what they've decided to do with me."

Mary's hand emerged from under the quilt. "Come here, old boy." It was hard for her to speak, having lost control of many of her muscles.

Claude sat on the rose-colored ottoman next to her.

"How you holding up?" Her words were slow and deliberate.

He looked at his bride of forty-six years. "They've worn me down some."

"You going to fight anymore?"

Claude shook his head. "Don't know. Hate to give up, but I'm not sure how much fire's left in me."

Mary slid her hand over his forearm. "You're a good man, Claude. Do what your heart says."

Claude fought back his emotions. He patted the wrinkled skin of her hand. "Maybe I need to spend more time here with you."

"That'd be nice, but do what *you* want to do. I've got no use for a grouchy man in the house." She smiled, pulled her hand back under the covers and closed her eyes.

Claude walked into the kitchen and filled the wood stove. He drank a glass of cold spring water then paused at the front door, staring at the key rack that had been there since they got their first car in the early fifties.

He lifted his town truck keys from the wrought iron hook they'd hung on for forty-five years and slid them into his pocket. He walked back over to Mary, kissed her on the forehead and left.

When he pulled into the parking lot at the town hall, no one was waiting at the door for him. He clomped the dirt off his boots and walked inside.

The building smelled of coffee, the fluorescent lights from the meeting room illuminating the leaf-strewn hallway. Claude approached the door and peered inside. Pelini, Harry, Reg, Tony, and Shirley were all sitting around the table, the remnants of a pizza on paper plates in front of them.

Claude turned the glass doorknob and stepped into the room.

"Come in, Mr. Demers," Chairman Pelini said. "Please sit down."

Claude kept his coat on and stood in front of the table.

"I'll get right to the point. In light of your many years of service to the town, we have decided to offer you a step-down position until you reach full retirement age next summer. We'll hire a new truck man and you can break him in. You will be prohibited from driving, but you can ride with him, show him the ropes." Pelini looked genuinely pleased, almost smiling as he waited for Claude's response.

Claude looked around the room at his friends, and then at Pelini. "So you don't think I'm safe to plow anymore?"

Harry fidgeted in his seat. "Well, Claude, that's not—"

Pelini cut him off. "That's correct, Claude, but we feel you can do a good job training a new man. It will keep you on the roads until you turn sixty-five."

Claude took a step back from the group. He closed his eyes, saw Mary's face surrounded by her blue quilt. He reached into his coat pocket and pulled out the keys to the town truck. He fondled the St. Christopher medallion that had ridden with him all those stormy nights. He considered taking it off the ring but figured the new man would need it more than he did.

Claude leaned forward and reverently set the keys on the table. "I've plowed a lot of miles for this town, been out all hours of the day and night chasing snowstorms, cutting up downed trees, fixing culverts, you name it. Got an awful sore back and arthritis has set into my knees."

Claude shifted his weight from one leg to another. "While you was in your session, I spent some time thinking and realized I'm kind of tired. And now that she's pretty much bedridden, Mary needs me home more. I've got a big wood pile to split and, hopefully, more hunting to do." He looked at Harry. "And I can't be where I'm not safe."

Claude stood silently for a few moments then turned, walked out of the room and down the hallway. He buttoned his coat and stepped into the frosty night.

Chapter 10

Ties that Bind Us

Coventry, Vermont, Early May 1929

Virgil stepped onto the back porch, the soft floorboards sagging beneath him. A brisk wind swirled tufts of dry hay against the stone foundation of their farmhouse. He held open the torn screen door as Skinny, his arthritic mutt hobbled outside.

"Mir'um!" Virgil called toward the calving pen, where she'd headed before sunup. He let go of the door and it slammed behind him. He listened for Miriam's voice above the wind.

Hearing no response, Virgil started across the hard-packed ground, his damaged left leg ratcheting along at his side. It had been crushed by their tractor when he tried to push it off his young son eight years before. A good natured, red-haired boy who loved to drive their new tractor, Silas had lost his balance turning on their steep north pasture and, as the tractor rolled, hung on like the captain of a capsizing ship, fighting to keep it upright.

Virgil had been boarding up a foxhole in the chicken coop when he heard Silas scream. He dropped his hammer and ran from the farmyard, past the barn, beyond the brown-rimmed sawdust piles and steaming manure pit. Eyes wide, nostrils flaring, he gathered great strides crossing the hayfield to the pasture, where he found the overturned tractor, under which Silas' skinny dungareed legs desperately thrashed, the heels of his boots digging futilely into the rocky soil.

Gasping for air, Virgil fell to his knees, saw his son's chest being crushed under the tractor, his ribs snapping like a stand of young saplings. Virgil frantically squeezed under the tractor next to Silas, heaving up on the hot motor till he thought his arms would split. He wedged his left leg between the ground and the metal gas tank, forcing it up slightly so that Silas could slide free. Despite Virgil's desperate cries, his son didn't move. When Virgil's arms gave out, the tractor shifted and the cast iron flywheel trapped his thigh against a rock.

When Miriam returned from the market early that afternoon, she eventually found them. Screaming, she ran cross-lots to a neighboring farm for help. It took the farmer, his son and their draft horse to right the tractor and free Virgil. Then Silas, who by then had turned blue.

Virgil knew Miriam would never fully recover, and he couldn't forgive himself for letting his only son plow that God-forsaken pasture, which any farmer in his right mind knew was too steep for cultivation. But he'd been unable to restrain himself—or Silas. Every Montgomery for four generations had managed to get something of a hard-earned crop off that hill. It was a family tradition, an agricultural rite of passage. "Once you clear and de-stone a plot of land, by God you use it," Virgil's father had told him many times.

After Silas died, Virgil went back to the north pasture only once, to fetch the tractor, which he parked in the shed. He'd covered the dent Silas' body made in the metal hood with an old buffalo robe and walked away. Despite the hardship of not using it, Virgil had been unable to bear running the tractor again. After Silas, Virgil and Miriam had tried unsuccessfully to have another child. At one point, Miriam sought Doc Miller's opinion about her inability to conceive again. He said her womb could not hold another child as it was filled with grief. Ironically, that was a bit of comfort for her, though she felt guilty for not being able to bear children at will like her mother and sister. It wasn't for lack of trying, at least after they recovered from the initial shock. But over the years, love-making turned to frustration and despair. They could not bridge the distance that Silas' death had put between them. It was a relief, really, when *the change* came early to Miriam.

It had been eight long years since Virgil and Miriam laid Silas to rest down by the river, his lone grave marked by a white wooden cross and a primitive bench Virgil had carved from a fallen cedar. Just as Miriam and Virgil's faces had weathered more deeply than their years, the bench had gradually faded to a cracked gray patina.

Crossing the farmyard, Virgil felt a lick of wind up under the tail of his shirt. He approached the calving pen. "Mir'um!" he called out, opening the wooden gate. He heard a cow moaning in the corner behind a mound of hay. He and Skinny limped over and found Miriam cajoling a mother cow in a steady voice while she pulled purple placenta from the cow's uterus. Virgil stopped when he saw a small, dusky calf lying lifeless on the straw next to Miriam.

"I'm coming, Virgil," Miriam said over her shoulder as she patted the haunches of the exhausted mother. "Car ready?"

"Yep, checked the tires. Tread's thin but got a spare."

Miriam pushed herself up from her knees. "You brought a jug of water in case the radiator boils over?" With her hands on her thin hips, she bent backwards and stretched.

"I will," he said, staring at the dead calf. They badly needed the little bit of cash good veal would have brought. It pained him the mother wasn't healthy enough to deliver a live born. Like so many poor farmers left behind during the *Roaring Twenties*, Virgil hadn't had the cash to buy proper feed for a good six months. Understandably, business folks were gradually turning their backs on them. Even his childhood friend, Orville Mosher, owner of the grain store, had run dry of patience with the Montgomery's seemingly endless financial struggles.

Virgil stood next to Miriam, searching for something to say. He knew how it upset her to lose a calf, or any animal for that matter, and no one was better at bringing them out alive than she was. He shook his head knowing if they didn't get some help off the orphan train, the farm would be lost. Like several of his neighbors, Virgil felt the presence of the crowded poor farm not four miles away. He'd be damned if he and Miriam were going to end up there.

Miriam pulled the stillborn calf closer to its mother so she could at least lick it, then walked over and sloshed her bloody hands in the rain barrel under the eave. Her overalls darkened as she wiped her hands. "I'll put on a dress and we'll go."

Virgil nodded, knowing she was upset at the second stillborn in a month. "You did everything anybody could." He knew better than to lay the whole blaming-himself-for-the-poor-condition-of-the-farm routine on her. She didn't cotton to that kind of talk. "I'll bury the calf later," he said.

She nodded, swung the gate open and held it for him. "Come on now, we're getting a late start."

Miriam disappeared into the house. Virgil and Skinny walked to the pump and filled a couple of glass jugs with spring water. Virgil set them on the back seat of their damaged Model T next to a basket holding a small block of cheese and a half loaf of bread Miriam had packed for lunch. Skinny crawled onto the floor behind Virgil, who'd barely settled into the driver's seat when Miriam came through the screen door in a faded, blue-flowered dress that fell well below her knees. A tarnished brass broach, given to her by her French Canadian grandmother, hung oddly from the front of the dress. Miriam checked the back seat for the water and frowned at the sight of Skinny nestled beside Virgil's fishing poles. She climbed in and pulled on the dented door hard enough to make it catch.

"Must you bring Skinny?"

"'Course. Got a good nose for boys."

"And your fishing poles?"

"Never know."

Virgil lifted the spark advance lever and opened the gas valve. He pushed the starter button, and after a few groans the car sputtered to life. He gave it some gas and steered out of their dusty farmyard onto a gravel road lined with budding brambles, raspberry bushes, and an occasional lilac. He followed along several newly plowed, coffee-colored fields that lay along the Black River leading to the Orne covered bridge. He slowed as they entered the canted shadows cast by the arched hemlock beams. As the car's tires rumbled across heavily worn planks, he caught glimpses of the river below, its dark blue-black current calmed from its raucous spring run a few weeks before. Emerging back into the sunlight, Virgil gunned the motor and they rattled their way up and over the washboardy hill on the other side of the bridge.

They descended into Coventry Center where, in the middle of the town's tiny green, stood a Civil War monument. Topped with a handsome Union Army soldier carved from Vermont granite, Virgil considered it the finest monument anywhere in the nation. He saluted the soldier then motored past the wide porches of the dozen or so houses that made up the small hamlet.

Miriam admired the beautiful but bittersweet sight of a sagging clothesline, weighted down with a family's worth of wash, a luxury she'd longed for. Hanging in the fresh morning air was a line of white muscle shirts and faded cotton dresses pinned next to colorful baby clothes, dish towels, diapers, socks and sheets as big as sails.

They turned onto the main road toward Irasburg and the passage west over the mountains. The dent in Miriam's door prevented her window from rolling all the way up, and as they gained speed she pulled a straw hat tight over her head to keep her thin gray hair from blowing about her face.

They rode in silence for a few miles before Miriam spoke. "They'll be a lot of farmers, probably some loggers at the train today. *Barton Chronicle* said it may be the last one that comes this way. Farmers out west get most of the boys. Besides, gov'ment may put a stop to it. Said some legislators think it's slave labor."

"T'aint no such thing," Virgil said, looking to his left then turning onto the winding road leading over the Lowell Mountain Range. "Those boys are treated better than down in the filthy cities whence they come. Unless, of course, they act up like that Mexican we had."

Miriam straightened in her seat. "Don't mention that troublemaker to me. We treated him good and fair—he was stark crazy is all. Bad brain from all the liquor they said his mother drank." She shook her head. "Awful. They weren't even sure who his father was."

"Moonshine don't make you *that* crazy—a boy of ten dousing a haymow with kerosene and lighting it afire." Virgil clenched his jaw. "Would'a burned the barn if you hadn't been in the milking parlor and had a bucket handy."

Miriam shook her head. "And him letting our horse out 'the stall and running her off—" She stared out the side window at the spring fields along the road, bright green dotted with black and white Holsteins grazing in the golden haze of morning sunshine. "God don't make many evil ones, but I fear he was one of them." She looked over at the gas gauge, which she knew was unreliable. "You enough petrol to get to Burlington and back?"

"Prob'bly. Can coast once we're over the mountain."

The main road was rough from the torrential spring rains and three weeks of relentless sunshine since. Virgil gripped the wheel tightly as the Model T lurched erratically back and forth in the long ribbons of mud ruts as they made their way over Lowell Mountain. The engine smelled of hot oil after the long climb, and Virgil seemed pleased they'd made it without having to stop and add water to the radiator.

When they reached the valley on the other side, Virgil persuaded his father's watch out of his front pocket and held it at arm's length in front of Miriam.

"Eight-thirty, already," she said. "I fear we won't make it there in time."

Virgil urged the throttle toward the floorboard. Stones kicked up under the running boards as they gained speed. Miriam's forehead tightened. "Don't push it too hard lest we run out of petrol. I'm hopeful we'll have a heavier load on the way home."

"Yes," Virgil said, his countenance lifting. "I studied the orphan list last night. I think we can get two good white boys if we get there early enough." He frowned. "They's some Negros and Mexicans, too. Don't know what you'll get." He tightened his grip on the wheel. "Can tell you I ain't driving way to Burlington to fetch a couple of coloreds. Won't have Negro hands in our soil."

Flustered, Miriam gave Virgil a disapproving look. "You afraid of what the neighbors'll think? I couldn't care. This isn't the 1800's. If we don't take what we can get—long as they's good boys—we'll lose the soil we've got. Bill collectors won't give us no more leeway if we don't produce a good crop this summer. You and I can't do it alone."

Virgil kept his gaze on the road.

"As it says in the Good Book, 'The Lord shall always provideth what you *need*, not always what you *want*.'"

Virgil waved her off. "Mir'um, there you go again, making up them Bible passages to suit your fancy." He glanced her way, caught her forming a thin line of a smile.

"Why, Virgil Osgood Montgomery, I would never do such a thing."

"Damn Bible-totin' woman."

Despite the work of a steam shovel and bulldozer, much of the road was still gouged out. Up ahead, a wooden sign leaned against a milk can, 'DANGER' painted on it in large white letters. Miriam sat up straighter in her seat. "Best slow down."

The transmission whined as Virgil forced it into a lower gear. There was no clear way around, so he bore down on where the road was washed out. "She'll make it," he said, sounding only half convinced.

"I don't like this."

Virgil put his foot down hard on the throttle. "Hang on," he said as the car dropped into a gravel ditch, its undercarriage scraping over several large stones. The water bottles in the back clinked together. Whimpering, Skinny beat the floorboards with his tail.

"Good Lord!" Miriam braced herself against the dash.

With a steep river bank falling away on one side, Virgil steered back toward the good part of the road.

"Come on," Virgil commanded through clenched teeth, his blanched knuckles tight to the wheel. The front end jolted as they headed up a gravel bank like a horse rearing on its haunches.

Skinny let out a high-pitched moan as one of the water bottles slid across the seat and shattered.

"You'll kill us!"

As they careened back up onto the good roadbed, Virgil saw a pointed tree limb sticking out from the rocks. "Damn," he said, torqueing the steering wheel hard to the left. The sharp wood scraped under Miriam's seat gouging the right rear tire with a muffled bang.

"You've blown a tire," Miriam said.

"God sakes, Mir'um, I know."

She reached over and righted the wet lunch basket and gave a shaky Skinny a pat on the head.

"Get ever'thing out while I fetch the jack."

"We damage the undercarriage?"

"Ever'thing out, Mir'um. Hurry now."

Miriam cleaned off the back seat, including the pieces of thick curved glass from the broken water jug. Skinny cowered from all the commotion and Miriam had to pull him out from behind Virgil's seat by the scruff of his neck.

Virgil was quick with the jack—from plenty of practice—and soon had the rear of the car up off the gravel. He kneeled down, wrenched the tree limb free, and installed the spare, its tread even thinner than that of the flat. Just then the jack settled into the loose gravel, pinching his hand between the tire and the fender. He jerked free, skinning a peel of flesh off the back of his hand.

"Hold the car, Mir'um. Keep her on the jack."

Miriam leaned her slight frame hard against the side of the car.

His hand bleeding, Virgil quickly tightened the nuts. They pushed the car back onto the traveled portion of the road, and he took a quick look at the undercarriage. He reached in and pulled out a stone that was wedged near the transmission then climbed in and started the motor.

Miriam brushed the road dust off her dress and got back in. She took a cotton napkin from the basket and folded it into a bandage for Virgil's hand.

"No need," he said, advancing the spark.

"Virgil, you can't be bleeding all over. Now hold still."

He let his right arm relax toward her. While he continued driving, she laid a torn flap of skin back where it belonged and wrapped his hand tightly with the white cloth. She pulled a piece of bailing twine from under the seat and tied it around the bandage.

It was over an hour later that they made their way into Burlington. "Damn," Virgil said when he saw the time on the university's clock tower. He raced down Main Street toward Union Station, which sat on the shores of Lake Champlain. When they arrived, the railyard was choked with farm trucks, and men and women talking to young boys.

"Look at all them people," Virgil said, shaking his head. He watched a pickup drive by with two confused-looking lads bracing themselves in the back. Virgil parked then he and Miriam hurried through the crowd toward the train, their hearts sinking as they realized most folks were leaving with their white orphan boys.

By the time Miriam, Virgil, and Skinny reached the platform, the men in suits appeared to have finished their work and were escorting the few boys who were left back onto the train. Tired, thirsty and disheartened, Miriam and Virgil stood and stared. Soon, dark faces appeared like shadows behind the train's sooty windows. Appearing scared by all the commotion, Skinny stood tight to Virgil's leg.

A man with a clipboard walked over to them. "Are you folks looking for an orphan?"

Virgil nodded.

The man offered his hand. "Charles Longway, Children's Aid Society of New York. And you're...?"

Virgil hesitated then briefly shook the man's hand. "Virgil Montgomery. My wife, Mir'um."

"Unfortunately, you're quite late. We do have a few boys left, though probably not what you're looking for."

Virgil scanned the train's windows, stopping at the face of the one pale boy toward the back. He pointed. "What about that one?"

Mr. Longway shook his head. "You don't want him. Fourth train he's been on, poor child. He has only one arm and a gimp leg. He'd never make it farming." He pointed to a window in the middle of the train car. "Those two are healthy and have well-developed muscles."

Virgil frowned. "The Negro?"

"Yes. He's a bit skittish from suffering some abuse, but he's no trouble. The other's Italian. Hot-headed, but strong. He and the colored are friends."

Virgil crossed his arms and squinted. "Nothing else?"

Mr. Longway shook his head. "They went fast this morning. Never seen so many farmers come for the train. Probably 'cause it'll be the last one. Stationmaster said there were several dozen folks waiting before sunrise."

Virgil thought back to *their* sunrise—the moaning cow, Miriam's forearms streaked with dark blood.

The man motioned toward the locomotive at the front of the train. "We've been delayed while they fix a valve on the boiler. You can have a look at what's left. I've papers to sign with another couple then I can bring the boys back down for you." He walked away.

Miriam nudged Virgil, but he didn't budge. "What do you think?"

"I'll look at the white boy."

Miriam frowned. "The gimp? How's he going to plant corn?"

Virgil's face puckered. He wanted a boy like Silas, not *just* like him, but enough. "Have the man bring the white boy down and we'll have a look."

Miriam shook her head. Skinny watched her as she walked off. Virgil looked back at the train. The colored boy slid open the window and smiled at him. The boy's face was thoughtful, intelligent, his eyes bright and curious. Virgil looked away.

Shortly, Miriam returned with Mr. Longway, who boarded the train. They watched him speak to the white boy, who didn't get up from his seat. The colored and the Italian both stuck their heads out the window and waved to Virgil and Miriam.

Mr. Longway came back down. "He's too tired to get off again."

Miriam stepped forward. "*Any* of them got enough energy to get off?"

Mr. Longway looked at the bright-eyed boys in the window. "It appears so."

"I'll look at the Italian," Virgil said.

"Those two are friends from the Brooklyn ghetto. Might be good to keep them together."

"The Italian," Virgil repeated.

"All right." Mr. Longway climbed back up into the Pullman car, spoke to the boys, and then led them off the train. He pulled the Italian around in front of the colored boy. "Mr. and Mrs. Montgomery, this is Giorgio. He's nine years old."

Giorgio tilted his head and looked at them out of the corner of his eye. "You farmers?"

Mr. Longway took hold of the boy's arm and snapped him into a better posture. "The Montgomeries will do the questioning."

Miriam looked Giorgio in the eye. "You a hard worker?"

"Can be."

"Not a trouble maker?"

Giorgio turned and smirked at the colored boy behind him.

Mr. Longway interjected. "Giorgio has quite a sense of humor, but he's not been real trouble."

"Shake," Virgil said, abruptly stepping forward.

The colored boy stayed behind the Italian, who frowned at Virgil then shook his hand. He held the kid in a hard, sturdy grip and was impressed when Giorgio didn't flinch. Virgil looked him over then turned to Miriam. "What you think?"

Skinny whimpered.

Miriam stared straight at Giorgio. "We need help on our farm bad. We'll feed and shelter you but won't tolerate nonsense. We keep a Christian home."

"So you'd like to take him?" Mr. Longway readied papers on his clipboard.

Giorgio's shoulders dropped. He motioned to his friend. "Can Jermaine come, too?"

Mr. Longway looked at Virgil, then Miriam. Neither spoke.

"He's a good kid, better manners than me."

Virgil looked at one boy then the other.

"Well," Miriam said, "we *could*..."

"Mir'um!" Virgil snapped.

She fell silent.

Virgil motioned toward the clipboard. "Sign for the Italian."

The colored boy tugged at Giorgio's arm. Skinny let out a weak bark.

Mr. Longway quickly filled in Giorgio's name on the paperwork, and Miriam signed it. He looked at Virgil. "You'll need to sign, too."

"He don't write," Miriam said quietly.

"Got to make your 'X' then."

Virgil tentatively made an 'X' on the empty line beneath Miriam's signature.

"All right, then." Mr. Longway separated the boys and spoke to Giorgio. "Hurry. Get your satchel off the train."

Giorgio looked mad. The colored boy looked forlorn, lost. Skinny sniffed his leg and his thinning tail began wagging back and forth.

Giorgio took hold of Miriam's arm. "Jermaine and me been together since we was little."

Virgil swiped Giorgio's hand from Miriam's arm. "Off of her!"

Mr. Longway advanced toward Giorgio, who stepped back. "I didn't mean no disrespect." He climbed back onto the train with Jermaine. Inside, they hugged each other then Giorgio grabbed his bag off the seat and returned.

"Good luck to you, now," Mr. Longway said.

Virgil led everyone to the car where Giorgio climbed into the back seat which was still damp from the broken water bottle. Skinny sat on the floor behind Virgil's seat whimpering. Giorgio appeared afraid of the dog and stayed away from him.

As they pulled away, Miriam watched Giorgio put his face against the side window, obviously searching the Pullman for his friend, but he had disappeared inside the dark car. As they drove up the long hill out of Burlington, Miriam spoke to the boy. "Are you hungry? There's a block of cheese and a knife in the basket there. Be careful not to cut yourself."

Virgil felt a bit of relief at finding some help and wanted to get off to a good start. He thought of how much he and Silas had loved fishing together. "You like to fish, boy?"

Giorgio stared out the window at the granite statues and sloping green lawns in front of the university buildings. "Nah."

"Too bad. Some say I'm the best fly fisherman around. Could teach you a thing or two."

"Fish are slimy. Jermaine's the best fisherman. Caught more fish out of the river than anybody I know."

"That so?" Virgil looked interested. "What river?"

"East River. Brooklyn. Everybody on the wharf knows him—even the old guys. We grew up on the docks."

Virgil slowed as they reached the top of the hill where a panoramic view of the Green Mountains opened before them. "Wow," Giorgio said, looking at the mountain peaks still capped with snow.

Virgil turned into a filling station and pulled up to a glass-topped gas pump. "Best get a couple extra gallons lest we run out." An attendant in oily overalls and an airman's cap came out of a small brick building and pumped the gas.

Turning away from Giorgio, Miriam slid a dollar bill from a small cloth pouch pinned inside her dress and handed it to Virgil. He paid the man then looked back toward Burlington and squinted. "You think they's still there."

Surprised, Miriam nodded, a smile tugging at the corners of her lips. He turned west and headed back down toward the train station.

Giorgio sat up straight. "You going back for Jermaine?"

The car gained speed as they passed under the canopy of stately elms lining the street.

The blue waters of Lake Champlain stretched for miles to the Adirondack Mountains of New York State. "We'll see if what you say is true—best fisherman in New York City."

Giorgio's face lit up. He leaned forward against their seat. "You'll see." As they approached Union Station, he pointed at the caboose which was just leaving the rail yard. "There goes the train!"

Virgil turned south on a dirt road that ran parallel with the tracks. He quickly caught up with the caboose, though he had to push the car hard to catch the steaming locomotive up front.

Miriam looked alarmed. "Virgil, the train won't be stopping anywhere for miles. You'll surely wreck the car for heaven's sake."

"Hang on," he said, bearing down on the churning black steam engine. The engineer blew the shrill whistle as the train passed a crossing south of the city. Virgil pushed the spark advance as high as it would go. The car's motor strained as it pulled even with the locomotive. Virgil thrust his arm out the window and began waving.

"There he is!" Giorgio yelled, pointing at Jermaine, who was riding next to an open window.

Virgil blew the horn several times but its *Ahhuggha* was no match for the loud chugging and hissing of the locomotive. "Help me, Mir'um, wave!"

"Lord All Mighty," she said, half wondering if he'd lost his mind. "Sometimes the Lord commandeth us to do wild things." She and Giorgio stuck their hands out the window and began waving. Finally the engineer saw them and waved them off. Virgil stayed hard on the gas and they all kept waving and yelling.

Looking concerned, the engineer backed off the steam. The train came to a screeching stop at the edge of a field.

Miriam scowled at her husband. "Virgil Montgomery, they can arrest you for stopping a train."

"Never-you-mind," he said, reaching into the back for the canvas bag holding his fly rods.

"*What* are you doing?"

Virgil opened his door. "Come on, boy." Giorgio climbed out and ran toward the Pullman car. Jermaine appeared on the steps and jumped into Giorgio's arms.

For fear the authorities would soon arrive, Miriam slunk down behind the dash as Virgil strode toward the locomotive. He called up to the engineer, who angrily yelled back at him. Soon, an agitated Mr. Longway was off the train, standing with the boys.

Mr. Longway addressed Virgil sharply. "What in the world's going on here?"

Virgil stepped in front of Jermaine, whose face showed a mixture of hope and confusion. Virgil nodded to Giorgio. "The boy, here, says you're the best fisherman in New York."

Jermaine looked confused. "Pretty good," he said, glancing at Giorgio.

"You ever fly fish?" Virgil asked, swinging the canvas case off his shoulder.

"Yes'sir. Sometimes they let us in Central Park."

Virgil untied the canvas and rolled it open on the ground. He slid out an old bamboo rod and spoke without looking at the boys. "You want to come work the farm with Giorgio?"

Jermaine's eyes opened wide. "Yes'sir. Sure would."

"Well, we'll see who's telling the truth."

By then the engineer and conductor had climbed down to see what was going on. Miriam and Skinny had emerged from the Model T and stood behind Virgil. Even the gimpy kid was hanging out of a window, watching.

Virgil handed Jermaine the fly rod, turned and pointed at a maple tree thirty feet away. "I'll give you three tries to snag a leaf clean off that low-hanging branch."

Mr. Longway shook his head.

Jermaine took the rod from Virgil and studied the tree, shifting back and forth from one foot to another. The trainmen looked at each other and shrugged their shoulders. Then Jermaine pointed at the other fly rod still in the canvas. "I can do it with the good one."

Virgil frowned. "My Orvis? Nobody touches that."

Jermaine tested the flimsy camber of the bamboo rod then looked at Virgil. "I'll do it one try with the other rod."

Virgil was intrigued. "*One* try?"

"Yes'sir.

Virgil's face puckered. He sized up the tree branch, its bright green leaves not yet full sized.

The engineer bit down on a cigar wedged in the corner of his mouth. "That's crazy. Nobody can do that."

Mr. Longway stepped forward. "Mr. Montgomery, this is highly irregular. I don't think you—"

"One try?" Virgil repeated to Jermaine, who nodded. Virgil took a shallow breath. "All right then." He took the bamboo rod back and laid it on the grass. He carefully slid the Orvis rod from its padded sleeve, aware that Silas was the only other person he'd ever allowed to cast with it. As Virgil slid the tight-fitting sections together, he remembered the excitement on his son's face that day.

Virgil stood and ceremoniously handed the rod to Jermaine, who carefully closed his pink palm around the smooth cork grip.

"Give him some room," Virgil said, motioning with his arm. Everyone took several steps back. The locomotive let out a sharp hiss of steam.

Virgil watched as Jermaine settled his shoes into the grass, felt for the substantialness of the rod in his right hand, the braided silk line draped across his fingers in the other. He raised the rod and began practicing his casting motion, the line whipping back and forth in a smooth, glistening arc over his head. A high pitched whish sung above them as the silvery thread laid itself out in mid-air in front of the black locomotive.

Silent and motionless, Virgil watched as Jermaine took aim and casted toward the tree. Everyone leaned forward as the featherweight fly on the end of the line flew under the limb. Jermaine whipped the tip of the rod backwards, bringing the hook racing back up under a burst of tender leaves. The hook tore through a leaf, shredded flecks of green fluttering toward the ground. Jermaine reached out as high as he could and caught the line just above the hook.

Virgil, followed by the rest, bent in close and stared. There in the crook of the hook was a tiny skewered piece of green leaf. Obviously rejoicing, Giorgio grabbed Jermaine's arm.

"There!" the engineer exclaimed, pointing at the hook.

"I'll be damned," Mr. Longway said.

Miriam watched Virgil's face. His eyes remained wide open. After a few moments, he extended his arm and touched the tiny piece of leaf. He swallowed so hard his Adam's apple rose and fell a good inch in his long neck.

Virgil took a step back, seeming to ponder the situation. "Never thought I'd see the day," he said, shaking his head. He looked at Jermaine, who waited anxiously, his hand held tight to the Orvis rod. "Might as well get your things off the train. Need to get home before dark."

Miriam tried to control her smile.

"You'll have to sign another form. I'll be just a minute." Mr. Longway returned to the train.

The engineer quickly got back to business. "Show's over. Hurry it up, now. Long run back to New York." He climbed the steel stairs into the cab.

Jermaine respectfully held the rod out to Virgil and watched him pull it apart. Jermaine stood there as Virgil wiped the two sections along the front of his shirt before he slid them back into the canvas case.

Virgil motioned toward the train. "Do you want to come with us or not?"

"Yes'sir."

"Then get your belongings."

Jermaine hurried back to the train.

Miriam stepped over to Virgil, but she knew better than to say anything. He had to let it all settle in, like fresh cement leveling itself.

Virgil slung the canvas case over his shoulder. "I'll be in the car."

On the ride out of Burlington, Virgil seemed to be knotted up. Miriam was aware of the boys trying to contain their excitement in the back seat. It wasn't until an hour later when they approached the village of Underhill and saw the golden afternoon hue of Mount Mansfield that Virgil finally spoke. "Just went by Jericho. You know which famous Vermonter lives there?"

Giorgio sat forward. "Ethan Allen."

Virgil shook his head. "Good guess, but he's been dead over a century. Anyone else?"

No one spoke.

"Calvin Coolidge would be a good guess. Thirtieth president, and I don't mean to be disrespectful, but *Silent Cal* did less than nothin' for small farmers, overseeing the rich getting richer and the rest of us getting poorer."

Miriam hadn't heard Virgil conduct one of his history lessons since Silas died. How they'd loved to quiz each other, especially during their occasional drives. History was one of the few things that excited Virgil and got him to talking.

Virgil nudged his cap to one side and pointed. "Well, I'll tell you who lived right there on the other side of those hills. Snowflake Bentley, the farmer who figured out how to photograph snowflakes. Famous all over for it. Even got his photo plates in universities."

Miriam knew the Bentley quote that was coming next.

"Mr. Bentley said, 'Snowflakes are miracles of beauty; masterpieces of design never repeated. When a snowflake melts, that design is forever lost. Just that much beauty was gone, without leaving any record behind.'" Virgil nodded his head with satisfaction. "So Mr. Bentley figured a way to capture them for us."

Clearly tired, Giorgio and Jermaine seemed bewildered by the history lesson and didn't respond. Virgil fell silent and headed north, winding along the Lamoille River, avoiding the washed out section where they'd lost the tire. It was dusk when they descended Lowell Mountain back into the Black River Valley. As they pulled into their farmyard, the boys pointed as two scrawny, rust-colored hens scurried in front of the car. Virgil, Skinny and Miriam climbed out and stretched. The boys stayed low in the back seat, peering out the windows.

Virgil held the door open. "You coming out of there?"

Giorgio straightened. "Where is everyone?"

"Everyone?"

"People. All the people."

Virgil frowned. "This is it."

Miriam leaned in toward the boys. "You're in the country now. Come on out."

Skinny whimpered as Miriam took Giorgio's hand and led him out of the back seat. Jermaine followed close behind. She motioned toward the back of the house. "I'll take you to the outhouse then show you your room."

Virgil interrupted. "Boys'll help me with chores. Then the house."

Miriam nodded. "All right. See you inside after."

"Follow me." Virgil led the boys to the shed, pointing to the outhouse on the way. He had them each grab a pointed shovel then took them inside the calving pen. Jermaine started when the gate slammed behind them. Virgil walked them over to the dead calf which had been abandoned by its mother and was covered with flies. The boys recoiled at the sight.

"Dig a hole on the other side of the fence there, deep enough to keep the coyotes off."

Jermaine gagged. Giorgio turned away.

"Go on, now. Be dark soon. We still gotta' milk."

The boys reluctantly walked out of the pen. Staying close to the fence and Virgil, they struggled to dig a small grave in the hard-packed earth. When it was finally deep enough, Virgil dragged the calf into the hole and the boys covered it up. By the time they were done, Virgil was too tired to teach them to milk, so he sent them inside.

Miriam led the boys across the porch into the farmhouse, dimly lit by a few kerosene lamps that created flickering shadows on the walls. They peered around doorways as she showed them the sparsely furnished rooms then led them up wooden stairs to a hallway, which held a lingering mustiness. She pushed the door open to Silas' room, and the boys gingerly stepped in, each placing his satchel on a bunk bed: Giorgio on top, Jermaine beneath. Miriam removed a couple of framed photographs of Silas and his leather baseball glove from atop the bureau and slid them into the bottom drawer.

Miriam stepped back to the doorway and watched the boys for a few moments. "I'll be in the kitchen fixing supper while you settle in." She let the door close quietly behind her and listened for a few moments. They whispered about how creepy the place was and the sound of their voices made her smile. As Miriam descended the stairs, she felt a rare moment of joy in making a meal for a *family* to enjoy, not something to be quickly endured with Virgil.

In the kitchen, Miriam pumped water into a pot and boiled a couple handfuls of last fall's potatoes, carrots, and parsnips, then fried a few thin slices of chicken in an iron skillet coated with bacon grease.

After Virgil had finished chores, he came inside and they all ate at the drop-leaf table in the kitchen. The boys and Virgil seemed apprehensive and little was said during supper. The food quickly disappeared then Miriam took a tin from the cupboard and placed four dry cookies on a plate.

After they each took a treat, Jermaine finished the last crumbs and looked at Miriam. "Thanks."

Miriam nodded. "You're welcome."

Virgil stood. "Chores start at five; come in for something to eat at six-thirty." He put his plate in the dry sink and walked upstairs. Miriam heard his footsteps stop at Silas' room then the familiar squeak of that door as he looked inside. She knew he would not be happy she had moved the photographs and put Silas' baseball glove away, but these new boys needed a space of their own.

Giorgio looked at Miriam. "What's he mean, *five?*"

"Chores, in the barn. Got to milk the girls before they get too full."

"I ain't getting up no five in the morning."

"Sure we will," Jermaine said, pulling on Giorgio's arm. "Now let's get some sleep."

"Guess it can't be worse than burying that dead cow."

Miriam looked at Giorgio. "You boys buried the calf?"

"Yeah, it was nasty."

"Yes," Miriam replied, frowning. "I'm sure it was." She saw how dirty the boys' clothes were. "If you need anything washed, I'd be happy to do them for you."

"Thank you, Ma'am," Jermaine said. They left the kitchen and climbed the stairs.

The next morning the boys were groggy in the barn as Virgil showed them how to sit on a milking stool and properly wash the teats of a Jersey cow. As sleepy as he was, Jermaine listened carefully to Virgil's instructions while Giorgio slumped against the wall and fell back asleep.

It took him a few tries, but Jermaine got the knack of pulling on the teats and rhythmically squirting warm milk into the ringing metal pail. Virgil looked over at the sleeping Giorgio, shook his head, then took a dip of milk on his fingers and flipped it at him.

"Leave me alone," Giorgio crabbed, covering his face with his arm.

Disgusted, Virgil continued working with Jermaine.

Over the next week, Virgil stayed on the boys hard, fixing a leak in the shed's roof, repairing rusted barbed wire fences, and moving a pile of composting manure out behind the barn. He was particularly hard on Jermaine, partly because Virgil's inner conflicts wanted him to fail, partly because Virgil saw promise in Jermaine's work ethic and cooperative nature. Giorgio was sassy and goofed off at the slightest chance, but he was a white boy. Virgil gave him more leeway.

One hot afternoon Virgil saw Giorgio flinging a fork of precious hay at Jermaine, but it wasn't until Jermaine returned the favor that Virgil angrily crossed the barn floor and snapped at him.

Miriam was cleaning milking pails at the time and was not pleased with what she witnessed. Later, when the boys took off to get a drink from the well, she approached. "Virgil," she said in a firm voice.

He drove his hay fork into a thatch of hay.

"If you drive the boys too hard, we'll lose them."

"Nonsense." He wiped his brow with his forearm. "Where they goinna' go?"

"They'll run off. You never shoulda' had them bury that calf the minute they got here. Land sakes."

"Somebody's gotta' teach 'em. No reason they can't work like…you know."

Miriam softened a bit. "They ain't never going to be him."

Virgil leaned on the handle of the rake and ground a tuft of hay into the rough wooden floor with his boot. "It was just right between us."

"I know." She watched him for a few moments. "These boys are pretty good workers, haven't caused any real trouble. If we're going to save the farm, we need them. Especially Jermaine. You know he's the best worker we've had in a long while."

"Yes, Mir'um, but——" He pursed his lips and squinted.

Miriam's voice gained an edge. "Is it 'cause you can't stand he's Negro? That why you haven't planted the rest of the corn? You don't want that boy's hands in your soil? You want to send him off and just keep Giorgio?" Miriam took a step closer and looked Virgil in the eye. "Is that what you want?" She shook her head. "Virgil, you can't have Silas back. Only in your heart."

He turned away. "I didn't say nothing 'bout Silas."

"You don't have to. I see how you suffer. Like I do."

Miriam waited a few moments. "Tomorrow's Saturday. Why not give them a little time off? Have some fun."

Virgil set his jaw, gripping the hay rake so hard his knuckles blanched. When he had forced himself under control, he adjusted his badly soiled cap. "Time to milk," he said without looking at Miriam. He turned and limped out of the barn.

Virgil worked with Giorgio and Jermaine for the rest of the day, finishing up by having them shovel fresh manure from behind each cow into a rickety wheelbarrow. It was after dark when he brought the exhausted boys in for a late supper, after which they staggered upstairs to bed. Virgil, dead tired himself, followed soon after.

Miriam lit a candle on the kitchen table then went outside and drew water from the pump into a kettle. She warmed it with the lingering heat from the cook stove then washed the dishes. She dried the china plates, hand-painted by her grandmother then carefully stacked them back on a shelf in the cupboard. When she was finished, she hung her apron on the door and stepped out of the warm kitchen onto the back steps where a cool evening breeze brought relief to her sunburned face. The leaves on the tall maples in the farmyard rustled over-head. A half-moon reflected off a sliver of river in the distance.

Virgil's sleep was fitful, as unnerving dreams ran through his mind. Visions of Silas appearing from the river bank, tossing a baseball in the field with

Jermaine and Giorgio. Flashes of trying to catch the ball with the boys, but the glove on his hand—Silas' glove—was too small, no matter how hard he tried to pull it over his palm. He saw the boys calling to him to throw the ball. He could see their mouths forming words but couldn't hear them. Visions of the red Massey overturning haunted him. Over and over he tried to catch Silas as he helplessly rolled with the doomed tractor. Virgil was only vaguely aware of thrashing about in his twisted, sweaty sheets.

He must have finally fallen into a deep slumber for he overslept, which tickled Miriam. By the time he came down to the kitchen, Jermaine and Giorgio were already out of the house. Virgil parted the curtain and looked out the window as he took a couple gulps of black coffee. "Where're the boys?"

"Up early." She motioned outside. "Probably playing."

"Got work to do. And I told them to stay away from the bench."

"Virgil, you worked them too hard yesterday. And yourself. Best let them have a little fun."

He set his coffee mug on the table, grabbed his gloves, and he and Skinny headed out. He crossed the farmyard to the tractor shed where the boys liked to hang out. He looked at the dusty buffalo robe covering the Massey's hood, then, not seeing the boys, walked to the edge of the field beyond the calving pen. A light rain had fallen overnight, and the wet grass was quiet beneath his feet. Two sets of boot prints headed across the barren lower cornfield toward the river. Virgil followed after them and, coming over a little rise, saw them sitting on Silas' bench. He could feel his face flush hot with anger. His heart beat uncomfortably hard. "Damn, I told them not to—"

Virgil ratcheted across the field as fast as his leg would swing. Then suddenly he had a hard time breathing and slowed. "That's my son's bench," he said in a voice much softer than he intended. The boys couldn't hear him above the sounds of the stream. Virgil felt light headed and couldn't walk any farther. He collapsed on the ground. After catching his breath, he leaned back and supported himself on his hands in the soil, mercifully softened by the night rain. Skinny nosed his arm and whimpered.

Surprising emotions overtook him. Virgil knew Miriam had worn the cedar bench smooth, sitting there so many times talking to their son. Sometimes he'd stand silently behind the bench and hear her tell Silas about the height of their corn and the brilliant colors of the fireworks on the Fourth of July. She'd report on the summer's fireflies and smile when recounting the Mason jar Silas had used to catch them. That jar, with its dehydrated firefly bodies, had sat next to a potted Christmas cactus on their kitchen's windowsill since the day he died. In late September when the sumacs turned to fans of red and purple and orange, Miriam would relate the size of their pumpkins and the length of the deep-rooted carrots he'd loved to pull from the ground, rub on his shirt and eat like a hungry rabbit. She'd tell him how desperately she missed him and that they would keep on, which is what she knew he would want them to do. It was what northern border families always did.

Only once did Miriam ever take Virgil down to the bench to sit with her. It was a cold March morning the year after Silas died. The hard-kernelled snow covering the cornfield crackled under their barn boots as they walked to the stream, still partially covered with thin plates of ice decorated with delicate swirls of white frost. They sat beside each other and after a spell Miriam slid her arm across his lap and took his heavy hand in hers. She told him she took comfort in watching the current ripple over the smooth rocks, gradually carving its way under the lip of the bank. And that sometimes she dreamed she was fishing with Silas on a warm summer afternoon as trout snapped at gadflies on the surface of a clear pool. Virgil sat in silence, his gaze resting on the wooden cross marking Silas' grave.

As Virgil's musings cleared, he realized he was still sitting in their field. Though usually in control of himself, he felt like something was emotionally breaking open inside of him. He lifted his head and looked at the boys goofing around on the cedar bench. He saw the gently rolling field waiting to produce the corn crop they so desperately needed. Aware of his own failures, Virgil knew God had not abandoned him, but that he had disappointed God. He heard Miriam's words: "You best let them have a little fun lest we lose them, too."

He did not want to lose anyone else.

Virgil pushed himself up, kneeled next to Skinny, and uttered a small prayer under his breath. He struggled to his feet and slowly limped toward the boys, who were taking turns tossing stones into the stream. After a minute or so they sensed his presence, whirled around and jumped off the bench. Fear was in their eyes, which normally Virgil would have taken satisfaction in, but that particular morning it seemed hurtful.

Virgil stepped beside them, the boys motionless, not sure what he would do. He picked up a couple of flat rocks and skimmed one across the water's surface. It jumped the bank on the other side and landed in a stand of weeds. Skinny barked in approval.

He spoke quietly without looking at the boys. "We had a son—Silas—used to love to fish this stream. That's why I built the bench here." He paused and skimmed another stone. "Must admit, seems good to have you boys around."

Jermaine relaxed a bit. "What happened to him?"

Virgil dislodged another stone with the toe of his boot. He pushed the words out. "Lost him. Tractor accident."

"How?"

"Rolled on him. I was a damn fool, like my forbearers, trying to grow corn from a rocky hillside intended for timber."

Jermaine looked at him. "That's why the old red tractor's in the shed. You don't use it?"

Virgil pushed the frayed rim of his cap back on his head and nodded.

"Farming would be easier with the tractor, huh?" Giorgio said.

"Might." Virgil turned on his good hip and pointed at the fallow field behind them. "Time to teach you boys to plant, get your hands dirty. We're late on some crops." He and Skinny started walking back toward the farmyard. "Come on, now."

The boys seemed excited as they followed behind Virgil for a few steps then took off running ahead of him, trying to push each other over as they raced toward the barn. Virgil had them grab a couple of hoes, and they walked to the vegetable garden where Miriam was on her knees tying white strings above rows of sprouting pea plants. She glanced over at Virgil and the boys, but said nothing.

Virgil rolled the sleeves of his shirt up above his biceps. "I'll show you how to make a proper hill for planting. Need two long rows, dozen hills a row." He took his hoe and vigorously pulled soil up into a mound. He added a shovelful of seasoned manure, a handful of fine gray ash from a metal bucket and thoroughly mixed it all together. When he was done he'd made a nice round hill, flattened on top.

"Mir'um's known for her squash, cucumbers, and pumpkins at the market in town. Gotta' have the right growing conditions." He motioned to the boys. "Now let's you make some hills."

The boys took the hoes and set to work. Giorgio didn't like sticking his hand in the ash pail but quickly picked up the overall task. Soon he stood back and looked at a reasonable facsimile of what Virgil had made. Jermaine, however, was awkward with the hoe and forgot to shovel in the manure. Impatient, Virgil watched from a few feet away. "Pull the soil up toward you into a hill. Don't push it."

Miriam kept checking on Virgil and the boys from the edge of the garden.

When Jermaine had finally made a fairly acceptable mound, Virgil pulled a small paper bag from his rear pocket and unraveled it. He shook a few seeds into his hand. "For strong squash plants you got to set the seed the proper depth then tamp it lightly." Virgil supported the muscles around his bad hip as he knelt in front of the hill. He took his thumb and made several half-inch-deep holes in the dirt about a foot apart. "No deeper," he said. He placed a squash seed in each hole then swept his palm across the topsoil to cover it. "Lightly," he said, gently flattening the soil. "Don't want air around the seed, but don't want it smothered neither." He looked up at the boys. "Got it?"

Giorgio nodded. "Sure."

Jermaine looked apprehensive.

"Plant your own hills now." Virgil pushed himself back up and stood between the boys as they set to work.

Giorgio quickly popped his thumb in and out of the dirt. He dropped in the seeds, covered them, and was done with it. Jermaine knelt down and pushed part of his fist into the soil, making too big of a hole. He dropped two seeds into the indentation then covered it with several inches of dirt and flattened it with the heel of his palm.

"No," Virgil said, shaking his head. "I told you not to tamp it too hard. Use just your thumb, like I showed you."

Jermaine seemed anxiety ridden. "I never worked in a garden."

"Then pay attention. Giorgio's got it."

Nervous, Jermaine leaned forward to make another thumb hole but lost his balance and fell into the hill, flattening half of it.

"For Christ's sake." Virgil took a step toward Jermaine then retreated. "Build the hill back up. Do it right."

"I'm trying." Jermaine made another hole with his thumb and, with his hand shaking, dumped several seeds into it."

Virgil became increasingly agitated, shifting his cap all around his head. Skinny sat up and uttered a low growl. Giorgio backed away as Miriam stood up over by the pea plants.

"Hoe the soil back up. You can't plant where you fell on the hill."

Giorgio frowned. "He's trying. He needs you to show him."

Virgil glared at Giorgio. "Don't tell me how to teach a boy to plant."

"Don't be so mean. He's had a rough life."

"*He's* had a rough life," Virgil retorted.

Jermaine hung his head.

"Judas Priest," Virgil said, seeing Miriam out of the corner of his eye. "Do I have to do everything for you damn orphans?"

"Virgil!" Miriam said sharply.

Skinny dropped his tail and whimpered.

"Stay outta' this. Boy's gotta' learn."

Jermaine sat back on his haunches, dirty tears on his cheeks. He glanced up at Virgil. "I'm scared. I need help."

Virgil felt his forehead furrow into a deep frown. His breathing quickened. A battle raged inside. "I can't." He paused. "I just can't——"

"Yes, you can," Miriam said firmly.

Virgil turned away from Jermaine and looked toward the north pasture. He again heard Silas scream, saw himself sprinting toward his son. Virgil closed his eyes till the haunting images passed. Finally, he held his hip and knelt again in the dirt beside Jermaine. He pointed to the hoe and Jermaine handed it to him. Virgil gathered the dark soil back up into a hill and flattened the top. Jermaine watched closely.

"Like this." Virgil hesitantly slid his weathered palm over the back of Jermaine's smooth hand. Virgil was surprised by the warmth that flowed from

Jermaine's hand into his. He cupped their hands together and helped Jermaine dig into the dirt and bring up the wasted seeds. Virgil brushed the dirt off the seeds in Jermaine's pink palm then took his thumb and helped him make a perfect hole in the middle of the hill into which they dropped a seed. Together they smoothed soil over the hole then Virgil showed him how to tamp it. When they were done, he continued to hold Jermaine's hand for a few seconds. "That's good."

Virgil felt his hand tremble ever so slightly, an aftershock from the breaking open of his heart. He was so overcome with the sudden arrival of healing that when he stood, he staggered backward onto the manure pile.

"Lordy, Jesus," Miriam said softly, a subtle smile creeping across her face.

Virgil managed to stand. "You boys keep them rows straight, hills round and full." He started to walk away. "Don't tamp too hard."

Under Virgil and Miriam's tutelage, the boys worked the field all day, planting a dozen rows of corn after they finished with the hills of squash, cukes and pumpkins. By the time late afternoon came, they were all exhausted. Miriam went inside to make supper, and the boys went and washed up at the pump. Virgil stepped into the cool shadow of his workshop off the side of the barn. He breathed in the warm aromas of gasoline, oily rags, creosote, and Murphy's Crow Repellent. Virgil stood in the dark, leaning with both hands on the thick, marred planks of the workbench. After a minute or so, he struck a match and lit a kerosene lamp, illuminating the shop with yellow light. He looked at the shelf high over the bench, its thick grey cobwebs undisturbed for years. He reached up and swept his hand across the front of a cigar box, the sticky strands stretching until they silently snapped. He took hold of the box and slid it off the shelf. Tiny veils of dust and dirt fell through the light.

Virgil lowered the box to the bench and wiped a finger over the white owl perched in the middle of the cover. He felt his heart beat faster as he lifted the lid with his thumb. Sitting on top of some papers were two black and white photographs, their edges curled with age. The first was of Silas fishing on the river bank. Virgil picked it up and brought it closer to the light. Silas was smiling, his hand blurred as he held a small wriggling trout. Virgil remembered how Silas protested when he told him it was too small, that he needed to throw it back to grow bigger for another day.

Virgil set the first photo down and picked up the other one. He squinted as he brought it into focus. Perched proudly on their new tractor, Silas held the steering wheel with both hands. He had that subtle grin at the corner of his mouth, the grin he got from his mother that would melt you; talk you into anything. The grin Virgil had so missed, the loss of which had bled the humor from his life. Silas looked so small sitting on top of the red machine.

Eyes welling, Virgil touched his son with his thumb. A few warm tears coursed down Virgil's cheeks and dripped off his chin, dotting the dusty bench. He bent forward, holding the photo tight against his chest. He was barely able to stand, feeling he might collapse under his own weight. Virgil leaned against the bench with his other hand and worked to catch his breath. He cried out involuntarily, a sound he'd never heard before. After a while he righted himself, wiped his eyes with his sleeve and looked at Silas. "I'm sorry, son."

In that moment, Virgil's soul lifted. He took a freer breath than he had in years. He kissed Silas' image, placed the photographs back in the box and closed the lid. He slid the White Owl and its secrets back up onto the shelf exactly where it had been. He'd waited eight years to release the pent up power in that old cigar box. He knew his life would now be different, and he was certain it would be for the better.

Virgil looked toward the farmhouse where Miriam and the boys were waiting supper. He blew out the lamp and closed the shop door behind him. There was a new energy in his gait as he crossed the farmyard, climbed the porch stairs and walked inside.

After a dinner of boiled chicken and the last of Miriam's parsnips, the boys went back outside and batted stones with a stick, playing two-man baseball with the enthusiasm of an entire team.

Virgil cleared the dishes and offered to help wash, at which Miriam motioned toward the door. "Why don't you go out and play with the boys?"

Virgil pulled back the frayed curtain and looked out the window. "They're having good fun themselves. Don't need me."

"Suit yourself." Miriam took a steaming kettle of water from the stove and poured it into the sink. She rolled her sleeves up and plunged her forearms into the warm soapy water.

Virgil walked upstairs and soon returned with a yellowed baseball. He walked outside and sat on the steps.

"You keep score?" Jermaine called over to him.

"I 'spose," Virgil replied. "Here, try this." He tossed the ball to Jermaine.

"Great!" Giorgio said when he saw the ball.

Virgil watched them play, keeping score by making marks in the dirt with a stick. After sundown, when they could no longer see well enough to hit they called it quits and walked past Virgil into the house.

"Thanks," Giorgio said and handed him the ball.

Virgil sat on the steps and watched the moon rising over the freshly planted field. He heard Miriam put the dishes away, say goodnight to the boys then climb the stairs to bed. The boys' voices moved from the kitchen to the front room, where it sounded like they were playing checkers.

When the air became too chilly, Virgil gathered himself up and walked inside. By the light of a lamp, he took off his dusty shirt and picked up a moist cloth Miriam had left for him at the side of the sink. He was about to wash his hands, but then stood staring at his palms, still darkened with dirt from planting with Jermaine. He ran the cloth over his face and neck and ears, then set it on the sink and blew out the lamp. He climbed the stairs and turned down the short hall to the spare room where he had slept alone for years on a creaky metal bed with a hollowed out feather mattress. He hung his work shirt over the back of a wooden chair, sat on the edge of the bed and let out a sigh. Skinny curled up in his usual spot on the small braided rug in front of the dresser.

Virgil stared into the darkness for a few minutes then rose and walked down the hall to Miriam's room. He hesitated then turned the glass doorknob. The hinges squeaked as he opened the door. Moonlight coming through the window revealed Miriam's shape under the quilt.

As the door closed behind him, she started and sat up on one elbow. "Virgil, you all right?"

"Yes."

"What, then?"

"I don't know. I thought I should come."

"Sit down," she said, sitting up against the headboard. She smoothed the quilt and he tentatively sat on the bed.

She pulled her gray hair back. "What is it? You sick?"

He looked at the floor. "I'm sorry I've not been here for you, Mir'um. Grief overtook me."

Miriam listened intently. She looked as if she would touch his arm but didn't. He heard the boys goofing around with each other through the wall.

"After Silas died I said we'd lost all hope for the farm. You said that wan't so." Virgil hesitated. "I was wrong, Mir'um. Dead wrong."

"You were bereft is all."

Virgil nodded. "I just want to enjoy our farm again. It's all I've ever known." He looked at her. "And now… t'aint the same, but they's good boys and we've some hope. And maybe we'll find time to go fishing."

Miriam motioned toward his side of the bed. "You want to lie down?"

Without speaking, he stood.

She pulled back the quilt and fluffed a pillow for him. "First you want to wash those dirty hands of yours?"

He looked at the dried soil on his palms. "No. They'll be all right till morning."

Virgil lay down beside her, slid a hand under the white muslin pillow. Miriam pulled the sheet up over his shoulders. He lay motionless as she adjusted her own pillow and gently placed her hand on his back.

About the Author

S tephen Russell Payne is a fourth generation Vermonter from the Northeast Kingdom town of St. Johnsbury. Inspired during a visit to his seventh grade English class by Sheffield poet, Galway Kinnell, Payne has been writing ever since. He has published both fiction and non-fiction in *Vermont Life Magazine, the Tufts Review, Vermont Literary Review, Route 7 Literary Journal,* and others. Payne's first novel, *Cliff Walking,* was published in 2011 to excellent reviews. He has made many appearances in support of the novel and to raise awareness and funds for organizations working to end spousal and child abuse, particularly, *Prevent Child Abuse Vermont.*

In 2013, *Riding My Guitar-The Rick Norcross Story* was published. This is the fascinating biography of iconic Vermont musician, Rick Norcross, who still tours with his award-winning western swing band, *Rick and the All Star Ramblers.* Payne and Norcross continue to make joint appearances in support of Rick's music and to benefit *The Lake Champlain Land Trust.*

Payne is a graduate of Tufts University where he studied pre-med and English, receiving his masters in English in 1978. He attended medical school and completed his surgical training at the University of Vermont College of Medicine, where he has been a Clinical Assistant Professor of Surgery since 1988. He practices general surgery in northwestern Vermont, where he lives on an organic farm with his family. He also serves on the board of the *Lake Champlain Land Trust.*

Payne's next novel, the sequel to *Cliff Walking,* is due out next year.

The author enjoys corresponding with readers and welcomes invitations to book events and speaking engagements. Please contact him through his website, www.StephenRussellPayne.com.

Other Books by Stephen Russell Payne

CLIFF WALKING – A NOVEL
(ISBN 978-0615493626)

Set on the rocky and at times unforgiving coast of Maine, this emotionally power-ful novel shares a poignant story of loss and love that weaves together the lives of three desperately struggling people. Kate Johnson, a recovering addict from California, finally escapes her cruel husband, Leland, by tak-ing her artistic son, Stringer, across Canada to Winter's Cove, Maine. Francis Monroe is a famous local seascape artist who is haunt-ed by the death of his wife. When Stringer meets Francis, events are triggered that al-ter the course of their lives. *Cliff Walking* is an intimate, probing novel about the healing power of hope that can grow from shared

desperation. It is a powerful love story that evolves through the hard-edged redemption of its characters.

> "Stephen Russell Payne has emerged as a new voice in Vermont's impressive pantheon of creative writers, and a powerful one. *Cliff Walking* is a dramatic story of suspense, love, and redemption, written with clarity, passion, and great sympathy for, and understand of, all aspects of human nature."
>
> —Howard Frank Mosher, author of *Northern Borders*

RIDING MY GUITAR–THE RICK NORCROSS STORY
(ISBN 978-1482529272)

This fascinating biography of American folk singer, Rick Norcross, chronicles his amazing journey from tiny East Hardwick, Vermont, to sharing the stage with some of the biggest stars in music. A renown photographer and founder of both the long-running *Green Mountain Chew Chew Festival,* and *Rick and the All Star Ramblers Western Swing Band,* Norcross has proven to be a natural entertainer and an award-winning songwriter. *Riding My Guitar* is filled with extraordinary stories from Rick's life—often humorous, sometimes heart-breaking—but always steeped in his love of Vermont's iconic history.

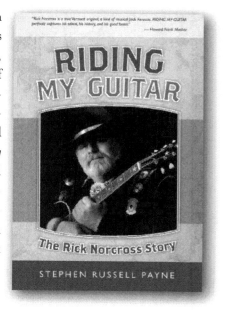

> "This book is the entertaining story of a true Vermont original. It's a fun read!"
>
> —Tom Slayton, *Editor Emeritus, Vermont Life Magazine.*

"*Riding My Guitar* is an engaging tale of an authentic Vermont talent. Rick Norcross's gifts as a songwriter, performer, and photographer are eclipsed only by his generosity and warmth."
—George Thomas, *former Vermont Public Radio music host*

Books and e-reader editions are available through local bookstores or through Amazon and other internet outlets

Made in the USA
Charleston, SC
02 January 2017